Promised to the Queen

Barbara Winkes

ISBN: 978-1-7781247-4-7

Created with Atticus

For D.

Prologue

Mia

Back then, I was still naïve about so many things. I trusted that my parents would always have my best interests at heart, that they would want to see me happy. I thought that they were financially secure, and that they were making smart decisions for a business built on hard work.

Mostly legal. A big part of it anyway—I can't remember ever being naïve enough not to understand where much of that money came from.

I understood that families like ours, *connected*, were different, and that each generation had to do their part to keep traditions alive.

I had no idea how far those demands would go, or how many other subjects I'd been ignorant about. After college, I did work a few days a week in the family transport business, Leonard Logistics, learning the ropes. It would all be mine someday, so it made sense for me to know the ins and outs.

I'd been holding that job for a few years while also jobbing at my friend Lucy's resort, a retreat she had built for women only. The more time I spent there, a place a couple of hours outside of the city, the more I realized that trucks and shipping containers were not my passion. I loved being out in the fresh air, helping with classes and hiking tours, and even sometimes in the restaurant, if needed.

The mountains and lake had a calming effect that I never found in my office at Leonard Logistics, and I had yet to tell my parents.

Being an only child made it harder, and I hadn't found the right moment.

That night, it was the birthday of one of my cousins, and after the family dinner, a few of us went out barhopping.

Earlier that day, Lucy had told me that she would like to offer me a full-time position. While this was great news, I had no idea how to break it to my parents. I didn't want to sound ungrateful because I wasn't.

I couldn't see them hire somebody from the outside. Trust is clearly an issue for *families like mine*.

"What's with the sad face?" Sadie, one of my cousin Camilla's friends, asked. "Cam is going to move into the corner office on Monday!"

"That is awesome," I said automatically, and Sadie seemed satisfied enough with my answer, because another drink appeared in front of me. Wine. They had been drinking cocktails and doing shots for most of the evening. I was grateful they didn't make me join in.

Promotions and access to funds at a certain age, that was all part of the deal. Well, I hadn't heard my parents talk about anything other than I'd inherit the company someday, run it with a carefully chosen "partner." They started using a gender-neutral word after I came out to them a few years ago.

I looked past Sadie and froze when my gaze fell on *her*.

The woman was sitting at a table by herself. Her white dress that hugged her figure in all the right places, and her hairdo, a carefully constructed messy bun, might indicate that she was waiting for someone. However, she seemed perfectly satisfied to be on her own, with her own thoughts, as she sipped her Martini. There was something unreal about her, classic beauty like out of an old Hollywood movie.

I had been staring a little too long when brown eyes met mine. She held my gaze, her expression somewhere between annoyed and amused. I was unable to look away. She broke the contact first, but my heart was racing. It might be the amount of alcohol, and difficult decisions ahead, but I knew better.

I had been obvious about it too.

"Hey, why don't you go over there?"

I shook my head at Camilla. "Not feeling it tonight," I lied.

It was a relief that my generation had no trouble with me being attracted to women, not that anyone had said much. But Camilla and her friends had included this place in the barhopping schedule, and she noticed my interest.

"Come on, Mia..."

"We are here to celebrate your birthday. And your promotion." I raised my glass again, trying to ignore what a few seconds of eye contact with that stranger had done to my body. I shifted on my seat, trying to ignore the sudden heat at my core. A fantasy, nothing else.

I cast another glance at the table in the back, but the woman was gone. I shifted my attention back to my company.

"Have I even told you how proud I am of you?" I hugged Camilla close and then picked up my empty glass. "I'll just go and get myself another one of those, okay? Don't go anywhere."

As I made my way through the crowd, I couldn't help thinking how much of a relief it would be to leave all worries and responsibilities behind for a few hours, hot sex with a stranger, a night of sheer abandon. Time where I didn't have to think about Lucy's offer, Mom and Dad's expectations, my own fears of utter and complete failure.

I took the new glass the bartender handed me, a deep dark wine that would go perfectly with pizza...The fantasy could include some food and more wine afterwards...how late was it anyway?

I could have perhaps claimed that I'd been jostled by the crowd around me, but the truth was I was so lost in my waking dream I paid zero attention on my way back to the table, colliding with someone on their way out, the catastrophe unavoidable.

She barely made a sound, nothing more than an indignant gasp when I all but showered her in wine, the front of her white dress drenched in red. I slapped my hand against my mouth, shuddering, because in the lights of the club, the color looked like blood on the white fabric.

The woman who had been starring in my fantasy just seconds ago wasn't hurt though, she was clearly mad at me.

"I am so sorry," I finally found my words. I looked around for somewhere to leave the empty glass while I shrugged out of the tiny bolero I was wearing over my dress. "Here, please use this."

She slapped my hand away when I was trying to wipe at the stain like some hapless heroine in a romantic comedy. Not her fault, but I lost my grip on the glass, and it fell to the floor where it shattered.

"Again, I'm sorry," I repeated, as I managed to get my phone out of my purse. "Please, let's exchange numbers so I can pay for the damage..."

Unlike Camilla, I didn't have the corner office and the trust fund yet, but I was willing to pay for my mistakes.

She once again held my gaze in that completely captivating, devastating way, and then she said, "Forget about it. You've done enough."

Despite her irritation, her voice was warm, dark, sending an inappropriate shiver down my spine.

"Please."

She shook her head and left me standing. I had never been this emba rassed or turned on.

I thought this would be the last time I'd ever see her.

I had been mistaken.

Chapter One

Mia

I'm not going to cry. I owe it to myself to keep my composure, to guard at least this much dignity. None of what's going through my head when my parents confront me with their plan, is much dignified. I can't believe they are going to betray me like this.

I can't believe they would even consider such a thing, regardless of how desperate their own situation is.

I'm aware it doesn't look good. I overheard a few things at recent family dinners, even though the subject is only ever raised in hushed, embarrassed tones. It's not that their transportation business isn't doing all right, but they needed huge loans to get where they are now, and their lenders intend to collect. Soon.

It's not just money that the once so generous Moretti family is after, though make no mistake, they want that too. They think they could get a bride for their good-for-nothing son at the same time.

Not if I have something to say about it. Over my dead body.

Finally, I find the words.

"I love you, but there's no way in hell I'll marry Joey..." I let my words trail off when I see the alarm in their faces.

"Mia, no, that's not what we were talking about!" My mother sounds almost offended. "We would never promise you to that horrible man."

I am far from relieved. I didn't misunderstand when they mentioned my duties to the family, and how desperately we need alliances. They do. But I have a job that's not related to the family business. It might not make me rich anytime soon, but it's fulfilling, interesting, keeps me busy and pays the bills.

"Then what are you talking about? It's the Morettis that you borrowed most of the money from, right? How are you going to fix this?"

"Mia, you know that we weren't careless with that money, but it's all tied up in assets. I know you think we're old-fashioned, but families like ours have accepted that times are changing. Enzo Falcone has remained a good friend and an ally even though his parents are no longer with us."

"What?" My voice rises a few notches, again. "He *is* married!" Not an asshole like Joey, but still. Married. And I thought they'd heard me when I told them I was into women.

"His sister, Alessandra, isn't. And she'd be willing to agree to an arrangement that would help all of us."

I had a dramatic speech formed in my mind from the moment they started mentioning the words "debt" and "marriage" in the same sentence, but I would have never expected this. I open my mouth and close it again when no words come out.

Impossible.

"You understand we don't have a lot of time to get the Morettis out of our business," Mom says. "And it's so much more than that. If this goes wrong, we might go to jail..." She has tears in her eyes, pleading with me. Not fair. Who wants to see their parents in prison? Unless they are, well, criminals. I shake the uncomfortable thought. I am not naïve. I know where that money came from, and I know that the trucks and containers with our logo often deliver more than what has been disclosed in the custom papers.

Never would I have imagined...

"Mama!" Two can play that game. "I'm so glad you understand I'm a lesbian, but that's still an arranged marriage. This is ridiculous! I won't do it. I can't."

"What's so bad about that?" she argues. "Your great-grandparents were in an arranged marriage, and they were happy."

"If I'm not mistaken, he was also the one who dropped the last letter from our name to blend in more, so forgive me if I doubt his authority when it comes to culture and tradition."

"Mia, that's enough! We ask this one thing of you. It's about time you took responsibility and did your share for this family. Other generations did what they had to do, and we are no different."

For most of my life, I've known my parents as quiet and even-tempered. Them raising their voices now is a clear indication that their backs are against the wall, though I can't help thinking that I'm not the irresponsible one.

I could ask my boss for money, couldn't I?

And if Falcone is such a good friend, why couldn't he help them out?

If I get married someday, and that's still a big if, I want it to be more than a business deal, a last resort. I want it to be love.

"You chose each other!" I accuse. "Why don't you want the same for me?"

"This is our only hope," Mom says. Maybe this plan weighs on her, but not enough to dismiss it. "You'll get a lavish wedding. Enzo and his sisters will pay for everything, and we can keep the business in the family. For you, and your future children."

"You are delusional!" I'm tired and close to tears again. I drove right here after my shift only to have them spring this outrageous idea on me before dinner. "Do you really think the Falcones won't take their share?"

And what's wrong with Alessandra Falcone that she would agree to such a travesty? The heat rises to my face when I think of all the implications. This can't be happening, not to a woman of my age in the 2020s.

"They will be investors, but we get to keep the majority of the shares," Dad explains. "You won't have to worry about that." He casts a glance at his watch. "It will be all right. We should have dinner soon though. Alessandra is expecting you later tonight."

"What?"

"We'll send someone to clear out your apartment and get you everything you need," he promises, looking relieved now.

"Clearing out...?" I realize this was never about hearing my opinion. They aren't all that comfortable, but now the cat's out of the bag. Dinner. They're already moving on.

I don't know them anymore.

Do I still owe them loyalty?

Fuck. I can't do this. I wouldn't even know who I am any longer.

"Okay, let's have dinner, I guess," I say, my anger rising again when they smile in response. "Let me go freshen up first?"

I don't go to the guest bathroom, but straight to the front door. It's locked, and when I try the security system, access is denied. Through the glass, I can see a security guard standing outside the door.

It doesn't look like I'll be going back to my apartment tonight. I must find a solution, and soon.

Welcome to my world.

The last thing I want is to see my parents go to jail, or worse, have the Morettis send some of their knee breakers after them. I know these things happen. I don't believe we have ever stooped to such low levels, but I've heard stories about other *capi*. It's a big risk to take, but...marriage? With someone I've never met?

It would be more than a marriage of convenience. The Falcones might be friendly, but they are aware that if they pay off Mom and Dad's debts, we owe them. It's me who's going to pay.

In the 21st century? I can't wrap my head around that.

I'm still determined to find a solution, but I'm not foolish enough to think I'm going to find it tonight. At dinner, I drink too much, and I talk too much.

"Look, before we go there, you have other options, right? I can talk to Lucy..."

"No, don't do that," Dad says, sounding serious. "We don't know her like we know the Falcones."

"What about Kendall Mancini? She still invited us to the christening."

"Which will take place after the wedding. Mia, please don't make this any more complicated than it needs to be. It's the best solution for everyone. They'll keep you safe even if someday we might not be able to."

That gives me pause, even considering that my mind is muddled with shock and alcohol.

"What does that mean? Why wouldn't I be safe? And why wouldn't you be there—" I halt when they share a concerned look, but I find more words soon. "What else aren't you telling me?"

"Nothing. I swear," Mom says quickly. "You know that Joey has been after you since you were teenagers. He's not going to be happy, but there's nothing he can do once you're married."

I can't deny it. Once upon a time, our families were closer, well, close enough to make mistakes with big sums of money.

11

Joey has been a pain forever, and he has a hard time keeping his hands to himself. The idea of getting married off to him makes me shudder, and not just because I've stopped dating men altogether. He is not a good guy.

What's the alternative? Hiding out with the Falcones? They will have expectations of their own.

Their daughter, my future wife, will have expectations.

This is all too insane.

I met the younger siblings once, a long time ago, but I know virtually nothing about Alessandra, except that she's an artist. Reclusive. For a reason?

"They might come after you even after you pay them back." It's not a question.

"Let them," Dad says grimly. "The playing field will have changed. We've increased protection to be on the safe side, but this is one reason why we must move fast. It will all work out for the best, I promise you."

"I'm sorry we had to spring it on you like this," Mom adds. "We'll head over there in a bit and finalize the details, and I'm sure you'll feel better. You'll like her. And marriage isn't always about love at first sight."

What if that's exactly what I want for myself? Is it selfish to hold on to that idea when it's apparently up to me to save our business and lives, because otherwise...what?

There must be a way to get out of this without anyone getting hurt—or married.

—ele—

We are not poor—or at least I had thought so—but I can't hold back the gasp when I first see the Falcone estate. Someone might think it's naïve, but I haven't paid much attention to who's who in the business, or what exactly their businesses are. I know the Falcones deal in art, which apparently taught one of their daughters an appreciation early on.

The parents passed away a few years ago, of natural causes. One grandmother is still alive, and she's been advising the siblings along with an uncle. She lives on the property. They will all be present tonight.

And Alessandra. I wonder if she's feeling as nauseated with humiliation as I am. Probably not, because she agreed to the deal. I'm not sure about the fine print, but I assume the part of our business they'll get is worth more than what they will pay to Joey and his family.

I can't think of any other reason, because why else would she say yes?

I guess I'm going to find out soon.

When we walk up the marble stairs, I wish I had changed rather than keep the jeans and hoodie I was wearing when I arrived at my parents' home. What I intended as an act of rebellion now makes me feel wildly underdressed for what we are about to do, and my mind is swimming.

Maybe I'm lucky and there'll be more wine. A family living in luxury like this must have an excellent selection in their cellar, right?

The housekeeper opens the door to us, and after a friendly welcome, directs us to the library where my fate will be sealed.

My heart is hammering, but I can't turn back and run, not with Mom and Dad—and the Falcone's security detail—right behind me.

The double doors close, staff staying outside. At the table, there are Lorenzo and Isabella Falcone. They look much too happy for the occasion. Their grandmother is sitting next to Lorenzo, and the man next to Isabella must be their uncle.

She is standing at the window, her back to us. When she finally turns around, my jaw drops. I grab the back of a chair, the next thing I can get hold of, to steady myself. The vertigo subsides only slowly. The need to find a solution has just increased exponentially, because no, I can't do this.

Alessandra Falcone is the woman from the bar. Judging from the small smirk she gives me before schooling her features into a cool, impassive expression, she remembers me too.

"Let's get this done, shall we?" she suggests.

I think I'm going to faint like the heroine in a Gothic novel I seem to have become.

Chapter Two

Alessandra

"It's time," Enzo says, and with a shrug, I get up from behind my desk to follow him and Bella to the library. I could be elsewhere tonight, at my own vernissage in one of the galleries we own, but I rarely show my face at these events anyway. I detest the small talk and the mingling.

So, when my siblings, giddy with the prospect of more immense wealth, come to get me, I don't stall them. It's not that Mr. and Mrs. Leonard's act of desperation will provide said wealth to us, not directly. While their business is an asset, we could do with or without it.

Sure, it's a farce, this whole thing, but a costly one if we don't go through with it.

A very lucrative one, if all works out.

I'm not looking for love. Like small talk, it's not a concept I'm interested in. It's about guarding the interests of the family and the business. As much as I tend to scoff at those tropes, I will do what's necessary to keep it all together.

My future.

Making sure Enzo and Bella don't go overboard indulging. Protecting a legacy. Yes, while this idea might look laughable at first, it serves a purpose.

After all, my grandmother too reminded me that this is how things are done. Gender doesn't change anything. The fact that I'm not interested in romance basically lends itself to this plan, and Mia Leonard? Well, we're expecting her, so it looks like she, too, has the best interests of family and business in mind, which means not handing it all over to the Moretti clan.

Everyone except me takes a seat.

I step to the window, the one leading to the park behind the estate. I don't intend to watch their arrival, though I must admit I'm a bit curious.

Mia Leonard is younger than me, an only child. Well, we both have our challenges. This marriage is to keep up appearances, a safeguard against a hostile takeover on their side, access to unprecedented wealth on ours.

Maybe it was my grandfather's idea of a joke, though Grandma insists that he was a hopeless romantic. She claims he wanted what they had, for all his grandchildren. I don't argue with her.

I hear the footsteps, our guests walking inside, and the housekeeper introducing Mr. and Mrs. Leonard, and Mia.

Formerly Leonardi. A few generations ago, their ancestor intended to make his name sound more American. Not knowing the exact circumstances, I have no room to judge, though this family seems to have a hard time holding on to their pride.

Well, we are here to help with that in exchange for a signature that will change multiple lives in a heartbeat.

I turn around and...I don't give myself away, though it was close. Mia on the other hand is an open book, her emotions written all over her pretty face, her expression stormy. I instantly know that this transaction won't be as easy as everyone expected.

Foolishly, I did too, thinking she'd be just as calculating about it as I am.

For the business. For the family.

The last time I saw Mia Leonard, she emptied her glass of red wine on my dress, ruining it for good. I wasn't emotionally attached to it, but waste is another thing I hate, and I had just bought it a week before the incident. I stayed mad at her for some time, which is unusual, because grudges are for amateurs. It's not who I am. Her doe eyes and pleading gaze had been on my mind for some time, on occasion in an R-rated fantasy.

Not that it matters anymore.

I don't need a lover, but a reliable business partner.

At this moment, Mia doesn't look like she wants to be either one to me. The way she is dressed almost presents an affront under the circumstances, on purpose, I assume.

Tough luck. Neither one of us can turn back now.

"Let's get this done, shall we?" I suggest.

Vincente and Flavia Leonard look relieved when they sit down after a round of handshakes. Mia's posture is tense. A bit dramatic maybe, but I can't help that twinge of sympathy. She's wound so tightly it must hurt, like she might snap any moment.

I wonder if the thought of what's to come is really so appalling to her. Getting married. To me. I think once the contracts are signed, I'll have to make a few things clear to her. Whatever she's afraid of, it's not going to happen. I'm not going to touch her, even though I've had a thought or two about it before I knew who she was.

"Whatever," she mutters, taking a seat next to her parents, the farthest from mine.

Have it your way, then.

"Thank you so much for coming." Enzo is happy to run the show, and the rest of us are happy to let him. It's also a feature of families like ours. "We have all the contracts set up, and I think

17

you've reviewed them already?" His gaze falls somewhere between the older Leonards. Traditions change. Slowly, but they do.

Mia still has little say in the grand scheme, but my brother can't ignore her mother. They didn't ask either one of us to marry a man. Small favors, right? The thought makes me smile, though I stop when I see Mia has caught me.

It's not for pleasure. I know where to find mine, and I'm sure she does too.

"We have," Mrs. Leonard confirms. "You've been very generous. We appreciate it."

"That should make Mr. Moretti back down," Enzo continues. "If he continues to give you trouble, just let us know, and we'll take care of it." He pushes the papers towards the couple, and they both sign.

"Can we get to the wedding already?" Bella asks, so excited I almost roll my eyes at her. If she wasn't already married, I'm sure she would have been thrilled to step in.

"In a moment, Bella. First, we have the most important papers to sign, so Mia and Alessandra can get their marriage license."

Strange how less than a decade ago, this would not have been possible. But it is, and we'll take from it what we can. I can make good use of this money. I'm sure Mia cares even less about the alternatives, though she stares at the paper with the same stubborn gaze.

For a moment, everyone in the room is holding their breaths, wondering if she's going to make a scene.

I'm not exactly worried, just slightly irritated that she's choosing this moment to stall the inevitable. What is her problem? She's going to get a lavish wedding, a life in luxury, protected from the unpleasant elements in our circles, like the Morettis.

I can continue to do what I love and still keep an eye on the mother company. A happy ending, isn't it?

Mia signs the papers, pressing the pen down so hard it almost pierces the sheet.

"Happy?" she says, addressing no one in particular, but I know the question is for me.

"How about a drink?" Enzo suggests, and he gets affirmatives from most.

"No, thanks," Mia snaps. "I've had enough."

"Mia," her mother scolds.

She doesn't argue, though her shoulders slump.

"I'm ready to call it a day too," I say. "Perhaps I can show Mia her quarters?"

Her eyes widen even though she must have known that she would stay here from now on.

Bella and her husband share a luxury apartment in the city, Enzo and his wife have a mansion of their own. Nonna and I have stayed in the family home, she, for sentimental reasons, I, because I appreciate the privacy.

There's more than enough space for two people in a relationship that's merely convenient.

If we keep our distance, disasters like at the bar are less likely to happen, and I can go back to concentrating on what matters, without her face constantly on my mind.

⸻ ℓℓ ⸻

For a moment, I worry someone will protest, drag this out longer than necessary. Mia's parents look like the reality of what they've done is now sinking in, reluctant to let her go. What are they thinking, that I'll ravish her in the hallway? That might have been an option at one point in our lives, but now we have wildly different priorities.

Mia hesitates, but she gets up and follows me outside of the room.

Despite the tense atmosphere, I suppress a sigh of relief when it's just the two of us. We'll have to establish some ground rules, and it will be easier that way.

Her demeanor changes the moment we've left the library, becoming almost demure. I'm not fooled. I've sensed the anger and resentment simmering barely under the surface, and I'm aware it's not entirely gone.

She speaks first. "Look, I'm really sorry about the dress. You were gone so quickly. I still want to pay for it."

So much for being demure. She doesn't want to owe me.

"Don't worry about it. You're aware all of this must happen fast, so we'll spend the next couple of weeks getting ready for the wedding. We can talk about your job once you're all settled in."

How's that for small talk? I meant to be reassuring, but I can tell from Mia's expression that I wasn't entirely successful.

"Job?"

Her voice goes up a notch.

"You know you can't go back to the resort. Don't worry, I'm aware of your qualifications. Once we've established how much of an active role we will play in Leonard Logistics, we'll find you something that interests you. But like I said, that can wait until after the wedding."

"I see." Her gaze drops to her feet as we walk up a flight of stairs. "You must be enjoying this."

I don't think her bitter tone is justified. We don't know for sure if Nonna is right, and our grandfather was simply that great romantic who wanted happy marriages all around in his family...or a calculating businessman who thought that this clause meant that we'd all work harder for the money. Bring only people into the family we can trust—or that owe us.

The two aren't always the same. Mia's resentment might lead her to vengeance, but I don't have the time or inclination to worry about that. This arrangement will make her parents' lives easier, and by proxy, hers. Sometime soon, she will understand that.

We put the Morettis in their place. Everyone can be, well, happy.

"I'm willing to do what's necessary to help my family," I clarify. "Aren't you?"

She doesn't answer, but at least she doesn't run away either.

We stop in front of the door that leads to a spacious suite overlooking the park.

"This will be yours. I'll have your clothes delivered here. You can either unpack them yourself or let me know if you need help."

"You're going to help me unpack?" Her tone is somewhere between amused and irritated, as if she can't settle on one single emotion.

"No. I'd send you someone from my staff."

"I see. So, we can't be living in sin before the wedding."

Mia looks shocked as if she can't believe she said those words out loud, as if she's given me an invitation. Did she intend to? I'm cautious. We can't complicate this situation any further.

Get the wedding over with.

Get her a job.

That's it, end of story for the two of us.

"I think we've all had enough for today. I'll show you around some more after breakfast tomorrow, and no, we don't have to share a bed, now or ever. It's not what this is about in case you were worried."

The blush to her cheeks is telling. So, she has given it some thought. For someone who grew up within some of the same structures as I have, Mia is startlingly naïve. I find it as endearing as it is irritating. The latter is not entirely her fault, it's the fact that I have a hard time pushing that first encounter from my mind, what could have been. In another life.

I open the door and let her go in first.

This is the best possible solution, far away from my own private rooms, and the ones I use for business, my office, and my atelier. Some doors are better left unopened.

"You should find everything you need for now. We'll talk more tomorrow."

When she closes the double doors, I step back and nod to the security guard who has appeared silently. Mia Leonard, soon to be Falcone, needs boundaries as much as she needs protection, not from me though.

I could use a drink now, but I prefer to have it in solitude.

My mind is still in complete disarray, and I can't have that.

Chapter Three

Mia

It's almost impossible to reconcile the woman from the bar with what I assume is the real Alessandra Falcone. Sure, they're both aloof and sexier than I'd like to admit, but when I first saw her, there was a warmth, a curiosity to her. Even after I ruined her dress.

Her being my future spouse, the one I didn't choose, makes everything so much worse.

She's judging me, maybe for my lack of loyalty to the family, my naivete, and under different circumstances, I would have given her a piece of my mind.

I can't do it, for various reasons. I'm still harboring the perhaps foolish hope that I might get out of this deal somehow. For that, I need her to be oblivious to my plans, or, the more difficult way, get her on my side.

I wait a few minutes, then venture back outside, only to have a polite stranger clad in black step in my way.

"Ma'am, can I ask where you are going?" he asks calmly, and without answering, I go back in, all but slamming the door in his face.

What did I expect? Mom and Dad had guards outside the door during dinner. Have they lost their minds, or are they really this paranoid?

I spend a few more minutes pacing in the surprisingly modern living space. It reminds me of a trip Lucy and I once took to Europe, where one of the hotels we stayed at was a renovated castle.

This is not a hotel though. It's supposed to be my new home.

I sit down on the bed, kick off my shoes and lie back on the surprisingly comfortable mattress, forcing back tears of anger and disbelief.

It's a nightmare from which I can't wake up, and it looks like I'm completely alone in it.

Alessandra doesn't want me. That should be a relief, but I have yet to feel it.

There must be a solution. I understand that Alessandra is a businesswoman—she can't be all right with being married off, especially by her younger siblings? There must be a way to reason with her.

A loud knock on the door startles me upright again, and I rush to open it. The guard is still there, a few feet away, watching closely as two men wheel in non-descript suitcases.

"What is this?" I ask sharply, angry and self-conscious at the same time. They might misinterpret the fact that I took off my shoes. I certainly didn't mean to make myself at home in this impossible situation. "Where are my parents?"

"They had this sent to you," one of the delivery men explains. "Clothes and other items from your apartment. They asked us to put furniture and everything you don't need right away, in storage. Here's the receipt."

I am both confused and furious. How could Mom and Dad let a bunch of strangers decide what I need?

"And here's your phone. Have a nice evening, Ma'am," he has the audacity to say before he nods to the guard, and he and his companion walk away. I remain in the doorway. The guard doesn't move.

On my phone, I find a message from Mom.

Thank you so much, Mia. This means a lot to us. Many opportunities will arise for you from it. We can't wait for your big day.

I look up from the text into the man's impassive face, knowing that nothing I say would convince him.

I walk back into the suite and slam the door once more, trying hard not to let the feeling of defeat set it.

Mom and Dad left? Just like that? I'm starting to wonder if they told me the entire truth. Yes, I know they borrowed from the Morettis. What are Alessandra's siblings, and maybe the quiet but attentive grandmother, holding over them?

I wouldn't put much money on the uncle at this moment. It's young, confident men like Lorenzo, and the elders, that run the show. The rest of us have to either wait our turn or work in more subtle ways.

I love my family. I've always hated being part of a connected family. Yes, it comes with privileges, but all this noise about loyalty and honor isn't just talk. You must keep the secrets. When you're asked to do something, you do it.

Except I've had a taste of a different life, my job with Lucy at the resort where people don't know and don't care about antiquated hierarchies. Oh, there's money, of course, and this is why I need to get in touch with her. I have two weeks. Maybe there's still a chance to turn this around.

I get back on the bed, and while forming plans to calm my racing mind, against all odds I fall asleep.

I wake up at dawn, shivering on top of the bedspread, disoriented for a few seconds.

I contemplate a hot shower, getting into fresh clothes. That would feel good. I don't want anyone, least of all, Alessandra, to think that I'm okay with this farce...but maybe I should. Maybe that could be my ticket out.

I am still confused. About how to help my parents without entering a loveless marriage, about my mixed emotions for her, about...I just can't stop, but I do know that I have to get out of this one way or another. Perhaps it would make sense to go along for the moment and not raise anyone's suspicions.

I finally take that shower and dress in new jeans, a t-shirt, and another hoodie. I put my hair into a ponytail. Sneakers in case I need to run.

There must be a way.

Before I leave the room, I step to the window and open it wide to let in the fresh morning air. It's a beautiful day, or it could be. I take in the vast space of the park behind the manor, then look down at the plants snaking up the wall.

There *will* be a way.

─ ℓℓ ─

Having decided that the execution of my plans requires caffeine and food, I'm heading down to the lower level. The guard doesn't follow me, so I assume every exit is secured. Maybe I should be afraid, but I'm mostly pissed.

It's bluster, a demonstration of superiority, nothing else. I can't help being the slightest bit impressed when I realize that this is only a small part of the entire home. The library isn't too far, but there are different wings. A private space for the grandmother, for guests, kitchen and dining, and Alessandra's, which I'm apparently not to see.

"Good morning, Ms. Leonard," a cheery employee in her thirties greets me. "I hope you slept well."

For someone who's been delivered by their parents, and is being held hostage, hey, not too badly. I don't say that, of course. Instead, I keep my tone polite.

"Thank you. I have to admit I have no clue how breakfast works in this house. Am I too late?"

"Oh n , don't worry about it. You can wait here, and I'll have your breakfast prepared for you. Everyone usually takes their breakfast in their quarters, but I'm sure they will join you this morning."

That makes me wince. It sounds like a bunch of lonely bitter people, never mind Lorenzo and Isabella being all giddy yesterday. But they don't live here permanently. Did they get to choose their respective spouses?

"Okay then. Thank you."

"What can I bring you? Would you like to start with a coffee?"

"Yes, please. I'll have orange juice too, pancakes, scrambled eggs, toast, and jam, and if you have, a strip or two of bacon?"

The door opens the moment I rattle off my list. I don't eat like this every day, and I do feel entitled. If they think I'm this obnoxious brat, they might send me home? Aware of my cheeks burning, I realize I don't want things to go that way.

"I like a young lady with a good appetite." A bony hand pats my shoulder, and I realize it's the grandmother, not Alessandra, who has just come in. Thank God for small favors.

"I think I'll have the same, Gina. And mix us some mimosas, please? It's a day to celebrate."

She winks at me, and I force a smile, unsure what to say.

Chapter Four

Alessandra

I love having my first cup of coffee at sunrise. By myself. It's the perfect way to start the day, and I need that time, but it will be a while before I have that privilege again.

Mia is not the only one who has to adjust to new habits. Having my first coffee with Enzo, who is the quintessential morning person, definitely requires an adjustment.

I have no choice. We have important matters to discuss. The planning of the wedding will mostly be in the capable hands of my enthusiastic sister, so I won't have to worry about that.

We need to demonstrate to Mia's parents that everything is under control, and that it's best if they interfere as little as possible. We save their business. Possibly, lives, but we don't need to be quite so direct.

"I don't know why you want to go over every little detail again," he says. "Cheer up, sister. You get a young bride and one third of five hundred million dollars out of it. That's a lot of money to put into one of your causes. We'll soon be billionaires!"

He's not wrong, and much too excited about this fact. He's also patronizing, and even given everything that is on the line, for all of us, I'm tempted to cut this meeting short. I wanted to give her some time and space, but I'm also anxious to find out how she's reacting to the new reality.

"We must have eyes on Joey Moretti at all times," I reiterate.

"Yes, and the old man, and their friends. I told you, it's done. Now, can we think about furniture for our offices at Leonard Logistics?"

There had better be bulletproof glass.

"You do what you have to do. Just don't be too obvious, and don't forget to update me twice a day."

"Yes, sis." He salutes, making me frown.

"Stop that. There might be no office. We have yet to see that any of us will have additional responsibilities there beyond our seats on the board. Let's go downstairs now."

"Can't wait to see her, can you?"

I glare at him, which shuts him up. For now. I, too, must be less obvious. I'll get over it, but my mind is still reeling. This is supposed to be a transaction, a convenience.

I can't have it mean more. That chance we might have had, that night, it's over.

I'm sure Bella is still asleep. She's a night owl, and has no doubt been browsing samples for invitations, but she won't emerge from her guest suite before lunch.

When Enzo and I get down to the dining area, I'm startled to hear laughter. I'm even more startled when I see Nonna and Mia sitting at the dining table, both of them having enormous plates of food in front of them. And mimosas.

"You are both late," Nonna chides. "Where are your manners?"

"Sorry," Enzo mumbles, suppressing a grin as we both take a seat, me across from my wife-to-be. I can't get over how young she looks in those casual clothes. I remember the dress she was wearing that night, the heels...Her challenging gaze.

30

The latter hasn't changed.

"Don't worry," she says. "Your grandmother was so kind to keep me company and entertain me with embarrassing stories from your childhood."

"She's a spitfire, this one," Nonna says, not confirming or denying Mia's statement. "You'll have your hands full."

Just like that, the atmosphere changes, back to awkward. Mia's cheeks redden as she directs her attention back to her plate. Pancakes. Bacon.

I have black coffee and a toast with butter. I feel her eyes on me the whole time.

She might be mad at me, but she has no idea how much worse her life could become. If it's up to me, she'll never know.

"Hey everyone!" Another surprise. Bella joins us fully dressed and awake. "I hope you can make time to look at some samples today. We'll get those invitations in just under the wire. I'll be fine once I have a color scheme to work with, and oh, I made an appointment for the cake tasting tomorrow."

Mia stares at her with a mix of awe and apprehension. I can't blame her.

Bella finally takes a breath, then continues to let our staff know her breakfast choices. A wholewheat bagel, low-fat cream cheese, a poached egg, fruit, and decaf. Without missing a beat, she returns to the matter at hand.

"Mia, your parents tell me they're going to have your great-grandmother's dress delivered. That is such a beautiful tradition. I'm afraid we don't have a legacy dress, but we'll find Alessandra something that will match yours. My friend is a designer, and she'll work overtime to get this right."

I can see Mia pale, and she sets down her fork and knife.

"Excuse me," she mumbles and gets up.

I follow her out of the room, hoping this won't become a regular occurrence. I can't watch her all the time.

Mia stops at the end of the hallway, spinning around to face me, angry tears glistening in her eyes.

I miss those early mornings by myself. I miss the time when I still had the fantasy.

"Damn it, can't you leave me alone for five minutes?"

I understand the feeling, but it's not up to us, not at the moment.

"What is it about the dress?" I ask softly. I reach out to touch her shoulder, and she steps back so quickly she nearly hits the wall. Dangerous. I'm sure she felt it too, that spark, that something she needed to get away from. My fingertips are tingling.

"Nothing. It's nothing of importance to you."

"I assume your parents have spoken to you about it before?"

"You bet they did." She leans against the wall, looking defeated. "What the hell is it that we are doing? You don't want this. You don't want me here."

I do and I don't.

"Don't make this more complicated than it is. You heard Isabella. She'll take care of everything. I told you that you'll have a job in the company as soon as we've settled the details with your parents. They are welcome here any time."

"But I'm not allowed to leave."

I consider lying to her, but I don't see the advantage in the long run.

"I don't think you're naïve, Mia. And if you aren't, you understand why we can't make any mistakes here. I promise you that you are safe as long as you're under my roof. Now go back to your breakfast. It's getting cold."

She scoffs but does as I say.

I hesitate for a few seconds before I follow her back. I intend to keep my promise, though it will require sacrifices from both of us.

They'll be worth it—or will they?

As promised, I show her around after breakfast. She's moping, but I am not fooled. I know she's taking in everything with a keen interest. Looking for an escape route, most likely.

I'm feeling the whiplash from all those mixed emotions, some tempting, some unwelcome—hers or mine, I'm not even sure. After we choose a color scheme of light purple and off-white with Bella, I all but flee to my quarters. In my office, I sit at my desk for a while before I get up again and walk to the room next door, a bathroom that connects my office space with my atelier. In here, I change into clothes more suitable for my real work, something that has little to do with the Falcone empire.

Sure, we deal in art, but a big part of that is a pretty surface. For me, it's everything.

There's a reason why I keep this part of my life hidden. The landscapes and still lives, that isn't a problem for my clan, or anyone we do business with. Tuscan hills, peaches and grapes in a bowl, I've been selling those under my own name.

Sela Andras sells a whole lot more, and not just because there's a mystery about her. All my models sign an NDA, and so far, it has worked. They enjoy what I have to offer.

Except lately, I haven't called any of them, and my latest sketches and drawings have mostly emerged from memory.

It looks like there is no escape for me either.

I stare at the woman who's staring back at me from the canvas, defiant, irresistible.

Mia will be fine, sometime soon when she understands all the implications, that this is the best-case scenario for everyone.

I will be...haunted.

Chapter Five

Mia

So, they are serious about all of it. I don't know all the details, but I can read between the lines. For the Falcones, this marriage seems to come with a lot of financial benefits, not all of them from my parents' business.

I'm still angry. What they owe doesn't seem all that much in comparison, given that Alessandra's family sees paying those debts as a viable investment.

That's all this is about, money, more money.

And she seems okay with it, living in this castle like the ice queen she is, doing...what exactly? She showed me some parts of the house, though there are others that are off limits for me. Her artsy rooms. Grandmother's space. The older woman is agreeable enough. I see no need to bother her. They won't have to worry about me sneaking around. I'm too busy thinking of ways to escape, every moment.

Except...I don't know what to make of it, that she came after me. To console me? There is no upside to this, no silver lining. Yes, I've known about the dress since I was five years old. When I was twelve, I exchanged my fantasy groom for a bride, but the rest never changed.

I wanted that dream wedding, with the fancy invitations and the centerpieces, and the four-tier cake. Wear a dress that has been in the family for generations, be a part of long-held, cherished traditions.

Be careful what you wish for, they say.

I'll have all of that, but it's worth nothing, because there is no love, just an ill-fated attraction I can't seem to get over.

Yes, against all odds, I'm still attracted to her, which is so much worse. Or is it? None of it is what I imagined my life to be.

I think about texting Mom, but I don't know what to say. I'm still disturbed that they left just like that, hours after telling me I was to marry a woman because her family could bail them out.

How real is that danger anyway?

I don't know for sure. I have heard stories about the Morettis, but then again, in these circles people like that a lot, stories. There's embellishment and exaggeration. I don't think Mom and Dad are prone to that, but they found themselves in a delicate situation. Maybe friends scared them? How would they come to take such drastic measures?

I still don't get it.

I still think of ways to turn everything around.

For the rest of the day, until dinner, I'm left to my own devices, though the guards stationed throughout the property don't budge.

In my bedroom, I take out my cellphone and call Lucy.

"What the hell is going on?" she asks without preamble. "Somebody from your parents' company came by to tell me you quit. I've been trying to call you!"

"Lucy, please, listen to me. I can't explain it to you in detail, not yet, but I need to ask you a huge favor."

More than employer and employee, we've been friends for over three years. This has to work out, because I don't really have a plan B.

"Are you in trouble?" I can hear her frown. "Mia, should I call the police?"

I nearly laugh at her question. Anything but that.

"I hate to say it but need to borrow some money. I swear to you, I'll pay it all back, and I will explain to you as soon as I can."

I'm certain about the former, whereas the latter...I'll have to tread carefully. Lucy knows about my parents' business, but arranged marriages and what ordinary people call organized crime, are not part of her world.

I hear her gasp a little when I name the sum, but to her credit, she doesn't waste any time.

"Whatever you need. It didn't sound right to me. But Mia, if I can do anything else..."

"No but thank you so much."

"Should I transfer it right away?"

"I'll meet you as soon as I can. Just please get it ready. I need it in cash."

This part is tricky. I'm not sure when or if I can shake the guards, but I don't want to leave an easy paper trail behind, for the Morettis, the Falcones or the authorities.

"All right. There's enough in the safe. This sounds ominous," she says somberly. "Are you sure I can't do anything else?"

"Just, please, have the money ready, okay? I'll call you when I can meet you."

I feel a little better when I end the call. I knew I could rely on her, and I wish my parents had talked to me first. I want to help them, but to be able to do that, I need to help myself first.

Before dinner, I unpack a bit more from the suitcases, to put everyone's mind at ease, and to take stock. The money exchange has to be as soon as possible, and I have an idea how to manage it. After that...I'll have options. I don't want anyone to get suspicious, so I'll go to the cake tasting with Alessandra and Bella as planned. In the meantime, I can figure out a way to approach the subject with them, offer Lucy's money as a form of down payment for the sum they have paid the Morettis.

I don't want to hang my parents out to dry. If Alessandra and her clan see that I'm serious about paying my dues, they will leave us alone, right?

Piece of cake.

As long as I don't think about it too hard. So many things can go wrong here, but I can't afford to worry much. It's all about money, let's leave it at that.

I'm not here to get to know Alessandra better—we had one chance, that night, and I blew it. Mom and Dad are right to some extent, I have to think of our family. There are better options than this. I'll prove it to them.

In the long term, Lucy is a much better partner in this, and what's even better, all of her books are clean. I know this because I helped her with them myself. Maybe we can bring her in as an investor, work something out with Alessandra and her family.

We might be all right, but first I'll need some time away, to think.

Time for dinner.

I don't want to raise anyone's suspicions by overcorrecting, but I feel like wearing something nice tonight.

—eee—

I didn't have to worry about dinner dress code or etiquette—it's quiet, just me, Alessandra and her grandmother, and the two of them seem lost in thought. Unfortunately, that leaves a lot of room for pre-emptive doubt.

Somehow, I can't take my eyes off Alessandra, her hand holding the wine glass, my thoughts inevitably wandering back to the bar. How much depends on this arrangement for her?

Why was she even at the bar that night? She doesn't seem like the type to enjoy crowds at all. In fact, I get the impression she felt crowded with her family and mine around.

I drop my gaze to my plate, my face heating, when I realize she has caught me.

"Do you need anything, Mia?" she asks. Most of the time, when she addresses me, her tone is soft like this, deceiving, infuriating. It's the right thing to put a stop to it.

I don't like being used, by anyone.

"I'm fine, thank you," I mumble, my cheeks hot with embarrassment. I could blame her for all of it, but I'm aware she's not responsible for my runaway emotions and libido. The sooner I can get out of here, the better. I will work around the clock for Lucy to make this right.

I *will* make this right, even if I have to talk some sense into Joey. Alessandra, more likely, because with the contract we have all signed, things have already been put into motion. I don't have much time.

I will not become a cliché.

Easier said than done I realize when an hour later, I stand at the window of my bedroom, now dressed in jeans and again, a hoodie. I'm up pretty high, but I hope the trellis will hold my weight. Otherwise, my story will turn from that Gothic novel into an absurd comedy.

I swing my legs over the ledge of the window and test the first step, putting my whole weight on it. So far so good. The rest is almost too easy, as I climb down, not even noticing thorns scratching my skin. In a matter of minutes, I'll be free—at least for a couple of hours. I can't run yet, or they'd be on to me too soon.

Once I've reached the grass, I run across the park where I find the almost hidden exit that I came across yesterday. It's not guarded, which tells me they never expected me to get that far.

Too bad.

When I'm out on the street, I head down a few more blocks until I call Lucy to meet me.

"Change of plans," I tell her. "If you could just bring me the money, and I swear I'll get back to you as soon as possible."

"I'll be there," she promises.

I hide in the shadow of a row of tall trees until her car pulls up, a BMW convertible. I love about Lucy that she gives freely yet isn't shy about letting the world know that she's a wealthy woman. It's the best combination, right? Unlike everyone else I know—including me, maybe. I've benefited from my family's wealth. With the gratitude for all those privileges, there was always a bit of shame mixed in. I'm ashamed now.

I sit in the passenger seat, and she hands me a duffel bag.

"It's in there," she says, and I can't help thinking that I'm doing the same kind of shady deal I know family members, the Morettis, and the Falcones have been involved in. But this is different. It's literally for the survival of my family and the business.

"Thank you so much. You have no idea what this means to me."

She gives me a stern, yet worried look.

"Are you in danger? You know what neighborhood this is?"

Oh, do I ever. Most people in town might be oblivious as to the whole story, but they are aware of the Falcones' incredible wealth. Even if there aren't indictments, there's always speculation.

"I'll be okay," I promise her. "I just need to take care of something. Give me a few days, and I think I could come back to work."

Lucy squeezes my shoulder. "You have my number. Please keep in touch. And not just because Nadja is certainly going to find out about the amount of money I took out of the safe."

"It will all make sense soon." I have high hopes for the both of us. "I'll call you, but I have to go now."

We hug briefly, and I exit the car and wait until she has left, then I make my way back. I've never transported this much cash like that, and wow, it's heavy. I sling the bag over my shoulder, feeling the burn when I start climbing back up the trellis.

I pray that the additional weight isn't going to make the whole thing come down. That would be beyond embarrassing, and likely painful, more than the scratches I get on my way up. When I reach the window, I toss the bag inside, wincing at the sound it makes when it hits the floor. Then I pull myself up and get inside, all of a sudden exhilarated. I made it!

Seconds later, I realize I rejoiced too soon. I nearly faint when I hear her voice.

"What the hell do you think you're doing?"

Alessandra is sitting in the armchair. I can barely make out her silhouette, but I know she's there, perfectly poised, not a wrinkle in her dress, her hair flawless.

I am still straddling the windowsill, probably have a couple of leaves in my hair, and I realize one of those scratches is bleeding.

I get all the way inside the room but stay by the window, my stance defiant.

Alessandra gets up, unhurried.

"What's in that?"

"No," I say sharply. "Don't touch that!"

Or else? She knows all I have are empty threats because she doesn't hesitate to open up the bag to reveal the stacks of bills.

She takes it all in before her gaze meets mine. I expected her to be angry, but up close I realize her expression is more curious.

"I suppose you have an explanation for this."

"I don't think I owe you an explanation for anything," I snap. "What? You're basically holding me hostage here. Are you afraid what I could do with a little money of my own?" The words keep tumbling out, much as I try to remind myself that I had planned to negotiate with her. I thought I'd be in a reasonably good position to do so.

My words seem to amuse her, a smile tugging at the corners of her mouth.

"*Cara mia*, I'm not afraid." The irony of her calling me this, and the intentional, somewhat cruel play on words involving my name...All of a sudden, my plan seems silly. More likely, she'll laugh at me.

"You're hardly a hostage, given how easy it was for you to sneak out. But we need to observe certain rules, and as you remember, we're picking our wedding cake tomorrow. You're right, you're entitled to money and space of your own, but until we have everything figured out, I think I'll keep this safe somewhere. You'll get it back once we've said I do."

"You can't do that!"

For a moment, I consider a crying fit, but of course that would only reinforce her image of me as a silly brat. I might still go there, but I need to be smarter.

With every moment I spend in this house, I realize this was not a spur-of-the-moment spontaneous decision for the Falcones. I don't know yet what that means, but I don't plan on sticking around long enough to find out.

"Oh, I can," she near purrs. Damn that woman for still having this effect on me. Everything could have been so much easier. We could have had that brief fling, that night, and I could have gotten her out of my system.

Something else springs to mind. Perhaps she never intended to get near me because she doesn't seem much interested now.

That night though...Why?

"You already knew who I was!" I blurt out. "You've been planning this since before that night?"

"I don't know what you're talking about." There's a hint of irritation to her tone now. "I didn't know who you were back then. While I understand that you have romantic ideas about marriage that don't fit the concept, we are making you and your parents a good offer. A much better one than you'd ever get from the Morettis, because I can promise you, I will leave you alone."

What if I don't want that?

The thought is as immediate as it is irrational. But I can't take it back.

"Yes, a really good deal. What are you going to do with that money?"

"Nothing. Like I said, I'll safeguard it for you."

"What if I don't want it? What if I pay you back for everything you paid to the Morettis?"

Her expression is sympathetic, making me cringe nonetheless.

"It's too late for that. You'll get this back right after you say I do."

"I already feel so cherished," I say, and I could swear there's a flash of hurt on her face, but it's gone in a heartbeat. Me getting distracted by Alessandra's flawless face clearly takes the sting out of the sarcasm.

"Have a good night," she says and leaves me breathless again.

With the anger and worry, there's something else mixed in that I can't have. That doesn't make it any less real.

Chapter Six

Alessandra

Part of me can sympathize. It's a lot to take in, for both of us.

Not that I was ever interested in the romantic and traditional aspects of the wedding and subsequent marriage that Mia seems to hold in such high regards. I'd be fine if we could just skip them. Go to the courthouse, make it official already, be done with it.

But Isabella insists we have a cake tasting to go to, so I made time in my busy schedule, even though I couldn't care less.

There's an exhibition coming up, and in addition to working at the company, I've been painting at night to get ready. What's worse, I'm distracted, by this new side project, by every pout and scowl Mia directs my way, by the fact that she generated substantial funds for an attempt at escape. Perhaps we need to have a conversation with Lucy.

Bella will knock on my door in precisely five minutes—she's never late or early—and I critically assess my mirror image.

Mia is resistant, stubborn.

Much unlike a number of models who couldn't wait to get in my bed. I shouldn't even have the sliver of an emotion about her reaction because any entanglement means complications.

Keeping the family business intact while making Enzo think it's all because of him, is enough of a challenge already.

We're a family with many secrets. I keep most of mine behind the doors of my atelier.

We are not heartless, and we understand the Leonards' situation.

I'm not entirely sure Mia understands, and until that is the case, I must tread carefully.

The knock on the door precedes Bella into the room. It's early in the day for her, so naturally she carries a coffee in a paper cup with her.

"Let's go!" she enthuses. "This will be exiting!"

Behind her, Mia is quiet, looking somber. She's wearing another jeans and hoodie combo, to show her rebellion or because she's holding on to a familiar comfort, I don't know. Next to her, I'm overly aware of the decade between us.

"Clearly," I acknowledge. "I have an hour, Bella."

"Wait until you see the place," she returns, and I swear I could see the hint of a smile on Mia's face.

Wait, now I'm jealous of my straight younger sister? The sooner we get back to a somewhat normal routine the better.

Something tells me normal won't be in the cards for some time with Mia under my roof. I can't even find escape in the canvases anymore because she haunts me even there.

We sit in the backseat of the car while Bella takes a seat next to the driver, chatting him up too.

Mia hasn't said a word to me yet.

If that's how she wants to play it, fine. Mia has no idea what could happen if she's alone out there with that kind of money, and I don't want her to find out.

Meanwhile, Isabella hasn't promised too much. The bakery is spacious and luxurious, situated over two floors of a historical building. It's a dream for anyone who is into cakes.

The owner herself greets us after hugging Bella.

"Thank you so much for choosing us," she says. "We have a room ready for you where you can look at the samples, and, of course, have a taste. How about we start with a glass of champagne?"

"Yes, of course," Bella says while I protest, "I can't. I have to work."

"Come on. We have a driver waiting."

I shake my head, and she shrugs. "As you wish. Mia?"

"No thanks."

The owner's friendly expression falters for a moment of confusion, but she's professional enough to move past it immediately.

"You can also have a coffee, juice, soda, anything you want. Just let me know."

"We will. Thank you so much, Diane."

Before we can get to any cake, my cell phone rings. Isabella looks disappointed, Mia annoyed.

Does either of them understand that our family name and business come with actual work?

"I have to take this," I mumble, and retreat to a corner of the room. It's Enzo.

"Target is on the move," he says. "Where are you?"

"About to start the cake tasting. I'll be right there."

"Stay put. I can handle it."

Maybe he can, maybe he can't. I don't have time to entertain his ego.

"I'll be there," I repeat. "Bella and Mia can finish up here. I'll see you in fifteen."

"Alessandra..."

I hang up on him and rejoin my sister, and my future wife.

"Something came up. I'm sorry, but I have to go."

Bella makes a face. "Did you put Enzo up to this? Come on, this is a once-in-a-lifetime thing. Well…We all hope."

"Funny. No, I can't stay. It's urgent. You take care of Mia?"

The latter is rolling her eyes at me while my sister finally understands the gravity of the situation. "Of course. We have it under control."

That's more reassuring than anything I have heard in the past week. Bella might be this bubbly, impulsive person, but she knows what's required. I don't have to worry.

Except now I do. I can't wait to get back to my atelier, but it will be a while.

I drive back across town to the headquarters. We are located close to a harbor, and today, Enzo is supposed to take care of a major shipment of sculptures from overseas. I hope there won't be any trouble, the thought making me nervous.

There's enough at stake, and I still have to take care of a duffel bag full of money.

I won't share Mia's shenanigans with anyone, hoping that will help me gain her trust, at least to an extent that we can have this working relationship. I intend to do exactly what I told her—safeguard it, which means I'll put it in a secret bank account I'll give her access to after the wedding.

If I put it in the safe, someone will ask questions, and I can't have Enzo thinking Mia might turn out to be a liability. I shake my head with a wry laugh. The whole thing was his idea.

If only he knew.

Of course, it's better if he doesn't know about the bar, and the frantic painting I have done since then. I have kept my eyes on him as I have on Bella since our parents passed away. Caution, obligation, it's part of the deal. Nonna is getting older, and she still has rather romantic ideas about how our grandfather ran the business. Uncle Paolo sits in on meetings, but most of it falls to the three of us. I believe it's better to be safe than sorry, so I hope he didn't mess up anything regarding the shipment.

Enzo waits for me in the parking garage, together with a woman I don't know.

"This is Lilly," he introduces her. "She has some interesting things to say about your bride."

Oh, that again?

"The one that you chose for me, remember?"

The woman named Lilly winces ever so slightly, and I wonder where he found her. My models, the ones I take to bed and the ones I only paint, are all vetted. I know from experience that Enzo hasn't always been as vigilant.

"Anyway, yes, but we have to be careful. We thought the Morettis were only lenders to the Leonards, but apparently the families have a long history. Lilly overheard Joey yesterday."

Yesterday? We have been keeping this under wraps, and I know that Mr. and Mrs. Leonard are more than grateful for the arrangement. How can they know already?

"He's not happy about your upcoming marriage with Mia," Lilly says softly. "He's planning something. I'm sorry I can't say exactly what that would be, but you should be careful."

"Lilly's risking quite a bit by being here," Enzo adds.

"Yes, and we're grateful, but we've employed every possible security measure."

I think of Mia sneaking out of her window the other night. I know that she got the money from her friend Lucy, but what if...No. Much as she hates the idea of our upcoming wedding, I can't believe she would take such measures to sabotage it. A lack of romance is not the worst she'll have to worry about if she gets entangled with the likes of Joey Moretti, and she's smart enough to know that. I have to believe it.

"Thank you for this," I tell the woman anyway. "I'll check in with Bella. She's with Mia right now."

"You found a cake yet?"

My glare stops Enzo from deepening the subject. Once again, I wonder how seriously he is taking this, or anything in life, for that matter. But one third of five hundred million matters to him, I'm aware. It matters to me too, if for different reasons.

"I would have if you hadn't called me away. Is that all regarding the wedding? I need to speak to you in private."

"I have to go," Lilly says, not waiting for an answer as she hurries to her car.

"Where did she come from?" I ask when she's out of earshot.

"Does it matter? Her information is always good."

He's irritated that I double-check. Figures.

"I assume you have a file on her. I'd like you to send it to me."

"Alessandra, it's not what you think..."

"Just do it. And while we're here, let's talk about the shipment. Are you expecting any problems?"

His expression becomes guarded. "No, why would I? It's arriving on schedule. We're good."

"Great. That's all I need to know."

At least something is going according to plan.

Chapter Seven

Mia

Alessandra leaving like this fills me with irrational disappointment, but it also lifts some of the pressure. It's like an alternate universe. Bella is nice, and the owner of the cake boutique is going out of her way to make us feel comfortable. She, too, seems a bit more relaxed without Alessandra around.

I finally agree to a glass of champagne while we sample the various options.

My dream wedding always featured a towering cake, and, for the longest time, two brides on top of it. I have to admit I never gave much thought to actual flavors. Buttercream? Chocolate? I wanted it to look elegant, for that once-in-a-lifetime event.

The champagne is mellowing me down, melting my resistance. I came here thinking that I might show my displeasure with the situation by choosing something outlandish, but it's hard to do that when everyone is so kind. Again, I wonder if Bella's marriage was arranged as well, and if they're just used to doing things that way. I guess it can work out sometimes...not for me, of course, but she seems happy. Serene. It's something I have yet to achieve, with or without Alessandra in my life.

I thought I was doing well at the resort. With regret, I think back to the offer Lucy made me. I had hoped Mom and Dad would come around, even though they always believed I'd come back to the family business full time. Is that even still an option? Alessandra said they'd find me a job.

I'm still confused, but the mix of sweets and alcohol is calming me considerably, for the first time since my parents broke the news to me.

If I can't marry for love, at least everything else will be exquisite.

"White chocolate and raspberry," I say, "I think that's the winner." Bella is smiling from ear to ear. I have the brief absurd thought that being in an arranged marriage with her would be so much easier, then I nearly giggle at the thought. She's a straight woman. I like her more than I should like any Falcone, under the circumstances, but it's not her I've had sweaty, lustful fantasies about.

My face heats, and I realize I need a break, a small moment to myself.

I can't forget that they're doing this for money and power, all of them. Alessandra took my money, Lucy's, to be precise, and God knows when or if I'll ever seen it again.

"I'd love another bite, but could you let me know where the restroom is first?"

"Of course. It's right down that hall," the owner points me in the right direction, and I get up, legs a little wobbly. Did I really drink that much, or is it just the magnitude of multiple decisions that other people have made for me? Well, at least I get to choose the cake, and perhaps the rest of the menu if Alessandra is too busy to take part in any of it.

I find the door without problem, about to go in when a voice behind me makes me spin around.

"Mia Leonard. Long time no see. How have you been?"

To see Joey Moretti in this place is surreal, the black-clad goon next to him only adding to the impression. Am I hallucinating? Having a nightmare?

"Really? I think you probably have a good idea. What is this crap you and your dad are pulling with my parents?"

The goon's hand goes to his weapon, predictably, his expression unchanged. Joey, however, laughs.

"You haven't changed, I see. You don't hold back. I always found that attractive about you. Look, I've come to put an end to this farce. I don't know what your parents were thinking by hiding you away from me, but this ends now. You're not going to marry the frigid bitch. It's making a mockery of tradition."

Even though I'm faintly aware of the potential danger, his open homophobia pisses me off. Him calling Alessandra names does too. Who does he think he is?

"My parents paid you back. Now leave me alone. I don't care for your opinion."

"They really did a number on you." He's still amused, but I can see something in his demeanor change, "Well, soon it won't matter. I can promise you that your parents are going to see reason. Come on, Mia. You and I have always belonged together. You know it."

He grabbed my ass once and tried to kiss me at a high school party where someone had spiked the punch. Come to think of it, he was probably the one who did it. I remember clearly that this was the closest we ever got.

"Get lost, Joey. I'm busy."

Done talking, he reaches out to grab my wrist and starts pulling me to the exit. I resist but stop when the goon draws his weapon.

"Let her go."

Bella's tone isn't so cheery anymore, and I had no idea she was carrying at a cake testing.

Multiple thoughts are chasing one another in my head. *We are all gonna die! Perhaps being married to Alessandra wouldn't be so bad after all, given the alternatives?* And: *This might be my chance if I play it right.*

But where would I go? Without the money Lucy lent me, everyone who wanted to find me would easily do so.

"That's cute," Joey says. "Ms. Falcone, I'm afraid we can't stay to chat." Goon raises his weapon, and several things happen so fast that I can only stare in awe.

Somehow, Bella kicks the gun out of the goon's hand, and Joey drags me with him. I hear the sounds of a fight and, more than ever aware of the stakes, tear myself away. He curses when I kick his shin and lets me go. I run back to where Isabella has the other man on the ground, training her weapon on him. Joey is gone.

"All right, that could have been worse."

Bella places a swift kick to the man's mid-section.

"Mia, take his gun," she commands.

My parents made me learn to shoot, and I'm halfway decent, but I never liked the feel of a gun in my hand. It creeps me out.

"Mia!" Her tone is sharp, and I obey. To the man, she says, "Get out of here. And tell your boss to never try anything like that again. He doesn't want to find out what we'll do."

Obviously in pain, he scrambles to his feet and limps away.

I am shaking, still holding the gun, still needing to have a moment to myself and pee.

"Where were we?" Isabella asks with a wry smile.

I owe my life to her. The realization makes me wobbly, and I reach out to steady myself against the wall.

She realizes that I'm shell-shocked and lays an arm around my shoulders.

"Hey. Mia. I think it's safe to go in there now, but I'll check it out first, and then I'll wait outside, just in case, okay? After that, we can finish up here and go home."

"Yes," I whisper. I walk inside the bathroom and lock myself into a stall, the past few minutes replaying over and over in my mind.

How naïve have I been?

Mom and Dad didn't make this arrangement with the Falcones because it was one of the options. It was the only option.

Joey has gone insane, and from the looks of it, his family will continue to indulge him. We desperately need allies, but laying my life into the hands of another person is a lot to ask.

I take care of immediate needs, get my breathing back under control, and I join Bella again, a smile plastered on my face.

"So, that was unpleasant, but I think another glass and another piece of cake will definitely help."

"Yeah. I spoke to Alessandra. She is on her way."

That gives me pause, my smile faltering. "You called her? Why?"

Bella looks confused. "Why? She needs to know about these things. We'll have to act so Joey and his ilk know this is unacceptable."

I don't want to ask.

"Besides, she's worried about you."

No, she's not, I almost said, but I keep the words to myself, and try to find solace in the sweet and the bubbly. No indulgence can hide that I'm still shaky, with anger, disbelief, and now that the danger is past, fear of the future.

I had dreamed of traveling once I had saved up enough money. I dreamed of so many things, but apparently the only thing remaining is the dream wedding. To a woman who doesn't love me.

She comes rushing in and, in a gesture completely unexpected, hugs me close.

"Are you okay?" she whispers in my hair.

I am in shock. Over Joey's behavior, over hers. None of this feels real.

However, the warmth of her embrace seeps into my body and mind, threatening my composure. I can feel my eyes welling up. No, this can't happen.

"I'm fine."

I wouldn't be if Bella hadn't reacted so quickly. How could she do that? Did they expect anything like this?

"Let's get you home."

Alessandra stays close to me, guiding me out of the store and onto the sidewalk where the driver waits on the curb, keeping a hand on the small of my back the whole time.

In the backseat, she holds me again, a rollercoaster of emotions making it hard to remember that she did take my money. I can't resist the feel, can't pretend it's not where I want to be.

Perhaps it's time to stop resisting. Perhaps I'll feel different tomorrow.

"I went with white chocolate," I say and, to my utter embarrassment, start to cry.

Chapter Eight

Alessandra

Mia is safe. Isabella handled the situation. I allow myself a moment of relief, though it doesn't last long. I don't envy Mia who will have to face some heartbreaking conclusions, and frankly, I should have been there. She is my responsibility.

I suspected that Joey might act soon, but not so soon. Crash the wedding cake testing? Nobody was supposed to know yet. There was a reason the Leonards rushed her daughter over from the family dinner.

Do we have a leak somewhere?

Equally as concerning is Mia's behavior, and my own. I can't deny how good it feels to hold her—relief, for sure, but is it relief for having avoided the worst-case scenario, or to finally have her there?

No. Don't exaggerate, don't panic. This is nothing like the fantasy that has been haunting me since she emptied her wineglass all over me. I promised I'd take care of her, like I'm taking care of the rest of the family.

Responsibility. That's it.

I keep telling myself that even when I accompany her to her room. She's still reeling from the experience, and on top of that, embarrassed and a bit tipsy. They really kept the champagne coming, no wonder given the cost of their creations.

"It's fine," she claims. "Go, take care of whatever you need to take care of. I don't need you to babysit me. I'm an adult."

"I know." Yet, I don't make a move to leave. "This was unexpected. It's okay to be a bit shaken."

She sits on the side of the bed, laughing bitterly.

"Bella wasn't shaken. You weren't. How fucking naïve have I been my whole life? Family. Honor. We are all such a cliché."

I fully expected her to use the f-word again, the thought making me smile despite myself. We are different. It's not just age that separates us. Thinking of the knowledge that seems to create a chasm, I don't feel like smiling anymore. There might be an advantage to Mia's way, trying to stay oblivious as long as possible, believing that all those dinners were really just a celebration of family, that no one ever got hurt.

I can't do that. Ever. I can only make the best of what we have now.

"We are what we decide to be," I tell her, and cringe. That sounds worthy of a self-help book, at best.

"Are we?" She raises clear blue eyes at me. They are welling up again. Alcohol and trauma are not a good mix. I step closer to her, and against my own better judgment, I take her hands. I can tell I caught her off guard, her eyes widening.

"For the past few days, everyone has been making my decisions for me. No one cares what I think, or who I want to be."

"Well, you did choose the cake," I remind her, my heart fluttering deceivingly when she laughs, genuinely this time.

"You are impossible."

Me?

I'm the one who's in this impossible situation. I can't afford this. I have...obligations. Yet I lean down and place a kiss on her lips. Soft lips, inviting me for further exploration. I straighten, aware of my rapid heartbeat.

Mia's gaze is stormy.

"You like messing with me, don't you?"

"I want you to be comfortable here. And I'll keep you safe. If you think that's messing with you, I'm sorry. I'll give you some space."

"No, wait," she calls after me. "You owe me an explanation."

I don't, but I wait at the door anyway, intrigued.

"No, many but let's start with the most important one. Did you anticipate anything like this to happen?"

Yes and no. "We've been monitoring the Morettis. They were not supposed to catch wind of our arrangement so early."

"So, there's someone in your organization you can't trust," she concludes. "Awesome."

"Hey. We don't know that yet, but we're looking into it. You keep forgetting all of this started when your parents couldn't pay back their debt to a bunch of criminals."

"We are what we decide to be," she throws my words back at me in a rather sarcastic tone. "A bunch of criminals."

"I'm sorry, but I don't have time for this conversation. I wish you could look at this a different way."

And then what?

She gives me a speculative gaze but doesn't comment.

I choose that moment for my escape.

I am busy for the rest of the day, setting wheels in motion, more precautions to make sure this is not going to be a *Game of Thrones* kind of Red Wedding.

I do this in my regular office, not the one connected to my atelier. God knows when I can return there. I can't be distracted by anything, until we are officially married, but it's getting harder.

Family, loyalty, love, all of it means pressure.

My grandfather's idea, romantic according to Nonna, or maybe just to mess with us two generations later? To leave his mark in all of our lives?

And our parents, how much did they know? For as long as I can remember, they kept a fairly low profile. Polite, even with us. They would have never gotten themselves caught in a situation like the Leonards did, and they knew that I was the least likely person to fall into a trap like this, hence...more responsibility.

Enzo and Bella, they do their jobs, and I couldn't be more grateful for Bella's intervention earlier. They don't carry the same weight. They never will.

And Mia.

I know it's not her intention to make my life infinitely more complicated, but oh, she does.

To my surprise, Nonna knocks on my door mid-afternoon, carrying a tray with coffee and cookies with her.

At the sight, I jump to my feet.

"You didn't have to..."

"You've barricaded yourself in here for most of the day, and you haven't had lunch," she argues, pushing aside some folders to set down the tray. "I wanted to see how you were doing."

I suppress a sigh.

The coffee smells amazing, and I know those cookies are homemade. I never even tasted the final choice of cake for the wedding. And still, she's not supposed to wait on me. I don't want to talk about how I feel either.

"I'm fine. As always."

"You still deserve a break. No one could predict what happened this morning, and Isabella knew what to do."

I give in and take a sip of the coffee, then taste the cookie. It's heavenly.

"It shouldn't have happened. I took precautions. If someone talked to Joey and his father, we'll find out."

Anger still wells up within me at the thought. But a lot of that anger is aimed at myself. From now on, whenever we have to leave the house, I won't let her out of my sight. At least I don't think Mia is inclined to run anymore.

The realization is strangely exciting.

"Yes, we will. And you have to remember it's not the same as what happened with—"

"Nonna, please."

"You'll have to face it sometime, *cara*," she says. "The days leading up to your wedding day are as good as any moment."

"I've faced what I had to. The rest is..."

"Just because there's a contract and money involved, it doesn't mean that you don't care about her. We all need to care about something, someone, but it makes us vulnerable too. It's smart to acknowledge that."

"Thank you for the coffee and cookies." I laugh a little. "I don't want to be rude, but I have a lot to do before dinner."

"I'll leave you to it, then." With a knowing smile, she adds, "One reason I came here is to let you know I'll have guests tonight. Since Lorenzo and Isabella are back home, it will be just you and Mia. It's overdue for the two of you to have some time to yourselves."

"You're not wrong," I agree, hoping she hasn't read my mind, the dizzying mix of hope and apprehension.

Her smile tells me my hope was in vain.

Chapter Nine

Mia

I stare at my wrist where a red mark still indicates what happened earlier today. He gripped me that hard. A stark contrast to Alessandra's actions, a few minutes ago, when she held my hands with such tenderness. Kissed me. My vision is blurring again, and I wipe a hand across my face, angry at myself and my mixed emotions.

It's over.

I can't ever go back. In any case, I can't run away before the wedding, because I'd be foolishly putting myself—and Mom and Dad, most likely—in danger.

No one withheld the truth from me.

What they told me, what Alessandra told me, it's true, and I've been blind to all of it.

My punishment? Being shackled to a woman who plays my emotions like a fine-tuned instrument, and I don't even know if that's habit, or if she enjoys it. I have to remind myself that her attempts at consoling me don't mean all that much, because she left me alone for the rest of the day.

Well, given how many times I've claimed I'm capable of making my own decisions, I could have simply gone to the kitchen and made myself a sandwich. Or ask someone from the staff to make me one.

The truth is I'm not even hungry, and I've spent far too much time obsessing on the feel of her touch and remembering her scent. Something subtle but undeniable. Figures.

I need to ask her about that job she's going to give me, because sitting around doing nothing will clearly make me lose my mind.

It's almost time for dinner, and I hope to spend some time with Nonna again if my fiancée can't be bothered. She's funny and fairly sympathetic. I could use that today.

It's mostly out of respect for the older woman that I take a shower to wash off all the scary, icky parts of the day and slip into one of my dresses. A loose bun will do, and I apply a bit of make-up. Needing to be in control of something, when apparently everyone has decided I deserve none. I complete the outfit with a pair of high-heeled pumps that I don't wear that often either. I'll have to take those stairs slowly.

As I stare into the mirror, I wonder what on earth has possessed Joey to think I was ever interested in him. That one time, I was a heartbeat away from throwing my drink in his face. I hope that my kick hurt, even though it wasn't as effective as what Bella did to that goon. I never thanked her either, the realization making my throat go tight again.

How is it possible to screw up this much? I am lucky that I'm still worth something to the Falcone family, otherwise I would be completely on my own.

The thought is terrifying.

I turn away from the mirror abruptly and head out, hoping to have dinner with the woman who reminds me of my own grandmother a lot, wise, serene, and funny.

I pause at the top of the stairs and walk down slowly, one foot in front of the other. The last thing I want is to embarrass myself by tumbling.

One hand on the banister, my gaze on the stairs, I teeter on my heels when I finally look up and see her standing there.

I've never seen Alessandra's gaze on me like that. Open. Revealing. There's affection, like earlier, but the subtext is an entirely different one. It makes my cheek heat. She just...stands there, as I'm walking down the stairs like some heroine in a romance movie. There I thought Gothic or horror would be a more apt term for the predicament I find myself in. I never imagined this sweet, exciting moment I created unintentionally.

Or did I do it on purpose? To test the waters?

I don't know anymore. I wanted a nice quiet dinner conversation with her grandmother, forget for a while that her allegiance, too, is to the Falcone clan and their goals.

"What?" I say, my defensive tone breaking the spell. Her guard is back up.

"Nothing. You're just in time. Dinner is ready. Are you...coming?"

A hint of amusement in her tone tells me she caught on to my predicament. I nearly slip out of my shoes and come down barefoot, but I resist the urge. Not in front of her.

I make it down to the main floor and manage to walk a bit faster.

"What's for dinner?" I ask. It doesn't look like her grandmother i. joining us, because...I stop again.

The dining room is set for two, complete with candles, and a carafe of wine. White wine, but if I had to guess, it is likely a Pinot Grigio. My favorite. I know it because the dish is seafood linguine, which is also my favorite. But few people know that aside from Lucy and...

"I called your Mom," Alessandra says, her voice warm as her hand on my bare shoulder. "Today was rough. I thought a little indulgence was the least we could give you." She pulls a chair for me, and, still stunned, I sit.

"I hope you'll accept my apologies." Alessandra sounds even more serious. "We will protect you better, I swear. This is one of the reasons we need to talk."

Only one? I hope she's not going to police how much of that wine I have, because I'll need plenty. I don't really want to talk, but I can't ignore that this setting fills me with something akin to hope. Stupid hope, and hopeless desire.

How can she go from acting like she doesn't care at all, to being all comforting, and back to polite strangers? I'm getting whiplash. Perhaps it's because I was slapped for real today.

I blink back those annoying tears that threaten again, too much emotion, and the scent of my mom's recipe doesn't help. I need to get it together. I'm an adult, about to get married.

"You're right, we do need to talk," I say, relieved that my voice is reasonably firm again. "First of all, you said I could get a job. I don't know what you've been told, but I've always paid my own way."

That is mostly true. I had a summer job in the company early on, and after graduating I split my time between my office there, and Lucy's retreat, spending more and more at the latter. I could have had a career there.

If that's out of the window, I need to know what my options are.

"You won't have to worry about money," she says as she pours the wine for both of us. "But sure, we won't let your talents go to waste either. Your family's business and ours are a good fit. I'll introduce you to the employees who will be working on projects with yours, and you'll be the best person to oversee that collaboration."

That silences me for a few seconds. She likes keeping me on my toes, and I definitely didn't expect that.

"What, you thought I was going to hide you away in a tiny office?" Alessandra laughs, the warm tone going straight to my...oh, damn it. I need to concentrate. Perhaps a tiny office far away from her is where I'd be safest, from everything and everyone.

"I don't know what I was thinking. Can you blame me?" I challenge her.

"Perhaps not," she admits, matter-of-factly. "I believe that you got the wrong impression about what all this is. We signed a contract that will help both our families. It will increase business for all of us. It will make everyone safer. That's a good thing, no?"

She holds my gaze long enough to make me blush. A few days ago, I had my own home, a job, and I was making all the decisions. How is it possible that this woman is reducing me to this awkward speechless mess?

"I suppose so," I finally say and take another bite of the tasty meal. I know she meant well with this, but it's another reminder of why all of it is so wrong. Neither of us can back out anymore, or can we? "Okay, so you want me to be the go-between woman. I think I can do that. I've worked with Lucy's partners over the years."

"Good. I had no doubts."

"Speaking of Lucy. I will have to pay her back at some point."

Alessandra nods in agreement, without awareness or admission of wrongdoing.

"What did you do with it?" The question lays bare all my mixed emotions about her, and her actions.

"Put it in a safe place, like I promised you. I will give you the details soon, you'll wire the money to your friend, and we'll close that account. You'll eventually have a regular business account, of course."

There's a tiny hint of impatience to her tone now, and I'm familiar with that too. Alessandra answers questions when she feels like it, and when she doesn't, she walks away. Is that what our marriage is going to look like?

A regular business account.

"You're unbelievable," I mutter and take another sip of the wine.

"I'll have to ask Flavia for more recipes. This is delicious."

"You don't have your own family recipes? Since you're so big on tradition?" I ask, genuinely curious. She's not offended.

"Well, by her own admission, Nonna isn't the best cook though she bakes delicious cookies. My parents both were excellent, but you know they passed away, and no one kept any hand-written recipes—or a family wedding dress."

Now, there's a rare hint of vulnerability to her tone, something that catches me off guard.

This time, it's not a sensual insinuation that makes my face heat. I crossed a line, and I feel awful about it. There's no reason to be malicious, especially given that I could have ended up in a much worse place today.

"I'm sorry. That was out of line."

"Well, you're not entirely wrong," she says. "I care about tradition. I care about what my family name stands for, and I'll do my best to make sure it continues to stand for the right things."

"The right things," I repeat. "I get that it's about money, but you can't be happy about this. You can't want this."

"That money is what might put the Morettis out of business, and for sure, it's keeping them out of your parents' company. It will assure independence for both of us."

She's not trying to convince me, I realize, just laying it all out. My romantic ideas for marriage have no place here. Why do I have to learn that lesson over and over again?

Today has taught me that things could be much worse.

Independence doesn't sound so bad, except in order to get there, I'll have to give it all up for a while. How long?

"That's one way to look at it, I guess. Okay. If we're in this together, how about you give me the details to that bank account now? Contrary to what you might think, I can handle my own affairs."

"Sure."

There's something about that little smirk that gets me going every time.

"Why do you think I can't? You don't know me!"

"Well...I know this. Your parents got in over their heads borrowing money from the wrong people. Your first impulse when things didn't go your way was ask your friend for more money. You can't fault us for wanting to keep an eye—"

"You know what, fuck it! This is never going to work if you continue to treat me like a child!"

I get up in a hurry, forgetting about the heels for a moment. I don't care anymore. I step out of them and turn to leave. I made it almost to the door when she catches up with me, spinning me around.

"What are you doing?" I snap. I get my answer a split-second later, when her lips are on mine, her hands on my waist pulling me to her, and the world disappears in this heated kiss. I let her in, and it's not because of anything that happened today, or in the past few days. I could continue to fool myself, but this is what I had been fantasizing about all evening until the moment I emptied my glass over her dress. Her hands are warm as they roam over my back.

I can't hold back the sound when her tongue slips between my lips, can't pretend I don't want this.

"You still think I'm not taking you seriously?" she asks, her voice now warm with undisguised lust, triumph glittering in her eyes.

I don't want any interruptions. I don't want to think this through, acknowledge how any step further could come with even more complications. I lean in, hoping she understands that talking is the last thing on my mind.

I sigh in relief when her hand is back in my hair as she's obviously satisfied with my non-verbal answer.

The next moment it's gone.

"Sorry to interrupt," Bella says, clearing her throat. Her blush leaves us with no doubt that she witnessed the kiss. "Alessandra, I need to talk to you."

"Yes." Alessandra is all business. I must have imagined the small trace of distraction.

"I'm really sorry about what happened." This time, Bella's apology is directed at me.

"That's fine. We were done. Mia, if you want, why don't you get a coffee and dessert from the kitchen? You can take it upstairs. Knowing my siblings, there's no saying how long this will last."

I force a smile. "Got it. I'll see you..." Later, I almost said, but I already know that Alessandra will always choose business over me. Hell, yes, I need something sweet, and forget about coffee. Wine will do just fine.

Pretending to ignore the hint of an amused smile on Bella's face, I pick up my pumps and leave.

Chapter Ten

Alessandra

I watch Mia walk out, desperate to make room between her and me. I can't function properly around her. One of these days, that could get somebody killed.

"Let's go to my office," I say.

On the bright side, Bella hasn't picked up on my mood. Then again, it's not good news either, because the reason she's here for is serious. Ever since Enzo came up with this idea, my siblings have been in and out of the house on a daily basis, and despite the vast space, I feel crowded. I long to go back to the atelier and lock myself in for a few days in a row, but under the circumstances, it's not going to happen.

"So, I guess we can agree that today was a shitshow," she starts when we are in the office.

I gesture for her to sit down, but Bella shakes her head. "I don't think we have time for that. Joey's not going away quietly. Take a look."

She produces her tablet and shows me a video. I am not new to this. I know how they operate, and yet the footage from a local TV station, firefighters struggling to save a structure about

71

to crumble, makes my blood run cold. I recognize where this is happening.

"We can't let this stand," I say.

Bella nods grimly. "Question is, how do we react? We still have some wedding preparations to do, and—" She holds up a hand when I'm about to protest. "This is important. We need to let everyone know that we're going forward as planned, that this will be a big, glorious union of two powerful families. There can't be any doubt as to who's in charge."

"I know all of that," I say irritably, casting another glance at the tablet before I hand it back to her. "Did you initiate the necessary protocols?"

"Of course. They have protection on the scene, and I've reached out to our police sources as well."

"Good. Thank you."

"You're welcome, Alessandra." Her tone softens. "I know you have a lot on your mind."

"Don't we all? You monitor the situation and let me know if anything changes. And I'll have Flavia and Vince over for dinner tomorrow."

"Tomorrow is a good time. They can come to the wedding dress fitting, right?"

How she can switch from serious business to her party planning is beyond me, but then again, that is serious business to Isabella too. Just as well—it means I don't have too much time to think.

Yeah, right. As if I haven't been thinking about her every minute of every day.

"I'll think of something. It's important that we don't do anything rash but send a clear message. Let me know what your police sources come up with. Thank you."

Understanding that she is dismissed, Bella nods.

I'm tempted to see Mia and let her know what happened, but something tells me it might be too much for one day.

The fire at her friend Lucy's resort destroyed a big part of the main building. No one was hurt—this time. I don't need to wait for the police report to know that arson was the reason, or who's behind this.

And they will pay.

—ell—

Coward that I am, I spend most of the evening coordinating our response with Enzo and Bella.

Conveniently, we got a tip about a shipment arriving tomorrow night. According to the customs declaration, there are tools and machinery in those containers—knowing Joey and his clan, likely, drugs. We'll have an alibi, the nice quiet dinner with my future in-laws to discuss specifics of the wedding, and perhaps some business.

"And after the goods have been seized?" Enzo starts on the conference call.

I shake my head, grateful that this is a secure line. "They'll be turned over to the authorities, as usual."

Sure, we could open up another stream of revenue if we got into that business ourselves, but it's the Morettis we are talking about. I don't trust their product, and besides, the drug trade is dirty, associated with a multitude of other lucrative but disgusting businesses. Speaking of what I don't want the Falcone name to be associated with.

In the long run we are better off knowing that there are a few high-ranking LEO's, prosecutors and judges that owe us.

They want to get the ones behind fatal drug overdoses, behind forced prostitution and sex trafficking, off the streets. We want to do business in peace. It's a win-win situation.

"As you wish," he says, and I swear there's a pout in his voice. So be it. Moretti is escalating, and we can't have that.

"All right," Bella chimes in. "Let's try some wedding dresses tomorrow. Mom and Dad would be so proud."

Would they be? I wonder every day.

—ele—

Giving in to temptation makes it worse. I avoided Mia at breakfast and went straight to work, focusing on everything that needs to be done today. The support we will provide to the local police department will only do so much damage to the Moretti clan, but it will hurt for a little while.

I'm good at this, minute details, put the right people and resources in their place, but it's hard not to let my mind wander. Mia...She's not letting up, not making it a secret that she's still holding out hope for the one thing I can't, won't, give her, to turn this affair into the romantic trope she is hoping for.

I can't seem to keep my hands off of her either, so we both need to be clear on what that means.

Nonna accompanies Bella and her friend Denise, the designer, to my suite. The latter has brought an entire rack with various choices, and I suppress a sigh.

We can't get the church wedding our grandfather certainly had in mind when he wrote the will he did, because in his mind I was likely to marry a man. Regardless, this is already going on too long, taking too much time. I wish we could just go to the courthouse and get it done, so we can all get on with our lives, but my family won't have it.

"I take it you haven't seen Mia's dress, but since she's going with a traditional choice, I think we should find you something that works with hers."

"Well, as long as it fits."

All that cheeriness is making me antsy. Nonna's eyes are bright. I assume she still thinks that our grandfather had romantic ideas about his grandchildren's marriages.

To my surprise, Denise's choices are thoughtful, appropriate for the setting. Formal, traditional, no frills—few illusions.

By dress #3 I'm ready to call it a day. I've been in predicaments before but being poked by needles while standing on a freaking pedestal is among the worst of it. Fortunately, I'm only doing this once.

I know Mia wanted to ask, but I can't give her a definite answer yet. This marriage will last as long as it needs to. That could be anything from a year to...

I suppress a wry laugh as I think of forever after with Mia Leonard. Falcone. It seems so unreal it's downright ridiculous.

In my walk-in closet, Denise helps me out of the dress and into #4. I cast a glance at my mirror image and freeze.

Much as I try to hold on to the thought, this doesn't look like a business transaction, like a pretend wedding. It's eerie. Disturbing. It's not what this is supposed to be, and yet, the woman staring back at me from the mirror looks excited, thrilled even.

"Wow," Denise says. "I guess that's the one."

No, I think. I can't make this such a big deal. Before I can react, she ushers me out of the room to meet the eager audience. Bella is clapping, and Nonna has tears in her eyes.

I look down at myself and suppress a sigh. The creation of silk and lace is a near perfect fit, though I envision some more poking. The color is a warm white, and I imagine it won't clash too much with Mia's family heirloom.

"I take it we're all set?" Bella says. "You look gorgeous."

"Thanks. I guess so. I mean, I have to get back to the office."

She laughs, aware that she got me flustered, which is a rare feat. But hey, this is my wedding. I don't intend doing it more than once, no matter what Mia's intentions might be some-where down the line.

The thought gives me pause, the idea that I might have to let her go at some point, causing a sharp pang of an irrational emotion. Then again, aren't emotions always irrational? A few days into this transaction, and I'm already in too deep. I can't go to that place again. It ended badly the last time.

I rush back into the walk-in closet, eager to get my regular clothes back on. Yes, I'll wear the perfect dress that one time, smile for everyone's comfort, and I'll take care of business. It's what I do.

Don't expect more from me.

Chapter Eleven

Mia

I don't know if I should be angry at Alessandra or feel sorry for her. I shouldn't be feeling anything for her, but here we are. I have breakfast alone in my room after finding the downstairs dining room empty.

There are still guards around the house, but they don't get so close now. I do find that some of the trellises have been removed from the wall under my window, and I don't think that's coincidence.

I am not thinking about running. First of all, I need my money back, and Alessandra made it clear that it's not going to happen before the wedding. You could almost think she's eager for it to happen.

Sarcasm doesn't help either as I eat my bagel with cream cheese, bacon, and a poached egg. I also got pancakes because I can.

My grandmother's dress fits me nicely. Isabella has invited her designer friend to help choose one for Alessandra, but I'm not privy to how it's going. She comes to check on me though.

"This is beautiful," she says. "It will go so well with Alessandra's."

I think everyone in this house has lost their minds. They're trying to do the impossible, use the old-fashioned ways to solve conflicts and consolidate business with a lesbian wedding? It's making my head spin.

But now that I've seen up close how far the Morettis will go, for Mom and Dad's sake, I'll have to go through with it. I wanted to wear this dress when I said yes to the woman I was madly in love with, who loved me back the same way, someone I wanted to spend the rest of my life with. My best friend, my partner in everything.

Instead, I've stumbled into a fever dream, lusting after someone who keeps shutting me out, who loathes showing emotion to anyone, including her future wife.

Emotions aside, she can kiss. Heat rises to my face as I remember letting my imagination run wild last night. Who could blame me? I am bored and worried all the time, and I have nothing else to do until I can go back to work.

Isabella notices my lack of response and gives me a long look I don't know how to interpret.

"I know you're having a hard time with all this," she says, reaching out to touch my shoulder. "But you're family now. You're safe here with us."

All I want is to be back in my apartment, and at the resort, doing my job. Perhaps that life was never really in the cards for me?

"I appreciate it," I say, though I'm aware it doesn't ring true. "I wanted to thank you." That, I do mean. "The past few days...I don't even know anymore. I guess it was never a secret that the Morettis are greedy and cruel. I had no idea that Joey was this interested in me." Even as I say it, the truth couldn't be more obvious. It's not about me, or my parents' money.

"You'll be fine," she assures me. "They will soon understand what they are up against." She takes a look at her phone after a small sound indicates a text message came in. "Oh, and your parents are here now. They'll be thrilled to see you like that."

If everyone is so happy, why can't I be? What more could I possibly want?

—ele—

Mom and Dad hug me close after they walk into the room. They have an air of caution about them, though I can tell Isabella was right. They are truly excited for me beyond the circumstances. Sure, I'm living in a mansion, getting ready for an expensive, flashy wedding to a gorgeous woman...That should make me happy too, shouldn't it?

I wish we weren't one of those families. I wish I could turn back time, but all I can do is try to make myself at home in the present. I missed them too.

"You look so beautiful," Mom whispers. "Grandma would have been so proud of you."

Pride, loyalty, tradition, do I even know what those mean? To me? To anybody?

I keep smiling.

"Just let me get changed, and we can go downstairs?"

It isn't until we all meet in the living room where Enzo is handing out drinks that I remember here is where Alessandra and I parted earlier.

Her smile for me is polite, not that different from the way she greets my parents, but I can't help thinking about what happened less than twenty-four hours ago. What almost happened. I catch her gaze on me, calm, a tad amused as if she's reading my mind.

Yet she insisted she was taking me seriously. I tear my attention away and listen to my mother talking to Alessandra's brother.

"So far, everything has been quiet," she says. "They've accepted the payment, and we haven't heard anything since."

"Sounds good to me," he replies. "Mia will help us to tie everything together business-wise, keep our employees up to date about your projects. I expect she'll work more from our side in the future."

"Of course, we expected that," Dad chimes in. "It's an exciting new challenge for her. You've been looking for that, right, Mia?"

"I wish I could have given Lucy notice," I say, alarmed when everyone in the room exchanges concerned glances. Alessandra's expression is impassive. "What's going on? What aren't you telling me? Is she okay?"

"Mia."

"I want to know right now!"

"Let's talk in private for a moment. We'll be back in time for appetizers," she says and takes my hand. Worry turns into fear as I follow her outside the room, struggling to keep up with her quick strides. Finally, she halts and turns to me.

"I need you to be calm," she says, hands on my shoulders, her words and actions making me the opposite of calm. "Lucy is fine, all of the women are. When we go back into the room, I need you to relax and let us all have a nice family dinner, all right?"

"What choice do I have?"

"There was a fire at the resort."

I gasp, slapping a hand against my mouth.

"It was contained," she insists. "We have our own security on site, and we are in constant contact with our police sources. I'm not lying to you. You can call Lucy to confirm."

"When were you going to tell me?"

She shrugs. "I was hoping to avoid it until after tonight, but that's not going to happen now. Rest assured that the problem will be taken care of. They're just acting out—"

"Acting out? People could have been killed! Lucy...Oh my God!"

"You're right," she says grimly. "This is why we can't wait until the wedding to deliver a blow to them."

"Okay. What is the plan?"

"For you, to have a nice dinner and be excited about the upcoming wedding. I promise you, by the time you sign your name, the Morettis will be done in this town."

My knees feel weak, and for once it's not because of Alessandra Falcone's presence or the way she touches me.

It's true: I can never go back. The realization is damning, sweeping away the last bit of hope I had this could be just a weird dream. They targeted my best friend. And before that, they targeted my family. It was likely never about the money my parents owed. Joey and his parents set them up. Because he's a rich spoiled brat, their only son, and what he wants, he gets.

Except this time.

"They're going to come after everyone I care about if we don't hit them hard," I say, hardly able to believe those words are coming out of my own mouth.

Alessandra doesn't argue.

"We have measures in place," she assures me. "Now, let's get back to dinner, shall we?"

"Yes. Let's do that." We're not done talking, but she doesn't know that yet.

─────ele─────

I'm reminded of everything I had conveniently closed my eyes to before, but that innocence—naivete—is lost forever. I feel

81

slightly nauseated thinking how much patience everyone had with me. I still dream of marrying for love, someday. Today I need to take responsibility for my family, my life.

I walk back into the living room with my head up high. Silently, I vow to make sure Alessandra tells me in detail what kind of protection they have in mind for Lucy—and those are not the only details I'll get out of her. She doesn't have to love me, but for the time being, she'll have to live with me.

"I think Isabella deserves a toast," Mom says, raising her glass. "She is putting the wedding together in record time, and it's going to be amazing."

One way or another. Yes.

I raise my glass with everyone else. They clink together lightly. Food and wine are plentiful, and I sense my parents' relief as they completely misunderstand the conclusions I've come to. It doesn't matter. I want them to be safe, and I'll take care of myself. One way or another.

There's a small, wistful part of me that wishes I could belong for real, in this family, with Alessandra...but we have bigger fish to fry.

—ele—

After everyone has left and Alessandra is about to head for her quarters, I hold her back.

"No. Wait."

She stares at my hand on her wrist as if taken aback that I dared initiate the touch. She doesn't pull back though.

"It's been a long day, Mia. I still have work to do."

"What kind of work?"

"Please, not now. We'll talk tomorrow, okay?" Alessandra is perfectly capable of making charming small talk for an evening, but her guard is back in place.

"You keep saying that, but we never do. I'm coming with you. Yes, now, because what I have to tell you is important."

She nearly sighs but is too polite to even do that. When she starts walking, I follow her, up the stairs, along the hallways, for the first time all the way to the place that has been taboo for me so far. Like so many things. If they want me to be useful in any way, I can't be oblivious any longer.

In front of the door to her private suite, Alessandra hesitates.

"I hope you don't think I'm the enemy here," I say. "I don't care if you didn't make your bed."

That makes her laugh, an unexpectedly joyous sound that also reminds me she rarely lets her guard down. Around anyone. Perhaps it's not just me, but this is not the time. My reasoning still stands.

Alessandra unlocks the door and steps aside to let me in.

She locks the doors in her own home?

I walk inside, finding nothing shocking in the spacious suite. The double doors to the bedroom are closed, but I catch a glimpse through the glass. What was I thinking? Of course, the bed is made.

I can't be distracted.

Turning to Alessandra who remains leaning against the door, waiting for me to start, I say, "I need more from you than reassurances. I've missed a lot over the years, obviously, but I want to make up for that. I need to. So please, tell me everything that's going on with my parents' business, and Lucy. I assume the Morettis started all of this even before money exchanged hands?"

She looks pained. I'm sorry, but I can't help it.

"Please," I say again. "I need to know what you're doing to keep them safe...and what I can do."

"I told you, our people are on it. Every single one of them is vetted. Your parents and Lucy will be safe, and so will everyone at the wedding. There's nothing for you to worry about."

Except one thing...

"I want you to show me around tomorrow. I have to know what I'm in for. Otherwise, people will think it's ridiculous that I get any position in the company."

With a shrug, she acknowledges it.

"You have a point. We can do that. What else?"

"I need to know how to defend myself. If I've been in the dark about many things, it's also because my parents sheltered me from a lot of uncomfortable truths—until the moment they told me I had to get married or else."

Alessandra winces at my depiction of the events, but at least she's listening.

"Something I've always known is that my parents care about the company. The resort isn't just about money for Lucy. It mattered to her to give those women a space to breathe. If you're going to make Joey pay, I'm in."

Silence follows, and I'm not sure what to make of it. Does she still not believe me?

I step forward, all of a sudden in her personal space, feeling like I crossed a line I can't uncross. I don't want to.

There's one last step to go.

I lean in, but before my lips meet hers, she has pulled me to her, her hold on me possessive, near desperate. "I will tell you everything you need to know," she whispers. "Soon."

Her kiss demands immediate attention, and I'm more than willing to give it.

Everything else...soon.

Chapter Twelve

Alessandra

It will be easy, Lorenzo had promised. *Parents got themselves in trouble with Joey and his clan. They need cash. The girl is working in some kind of resort where she lends a hand wherever needed, and I think...goat yoga? You won't even have to change your antisocial ways.* The last part, he said with a bit of admiration. People want to be his friend, but they fear me, and it's better for business.

There were no goats on Lucy's property, but that's beside the point. The "girl" turned out to be my fantasy woman from the bar, the one who snuck into my mind and onto my canvas, and she's everything but easy.

Mia wants to know details, as it's finally dawning on her that she's been in the dark for most of her life. Part of it might have been her parents' doing, another part...I can't remember a time when I had a choice between accepting or rejecting the Falcone legacy. I'm proud of what I do, and yet, some days, the urge to shut myself away in the atelier is almost overwhelming.

Now, there's one more person I'm responsible for, and it's already a lot more complicated than a simple signature that unlocks a five hundred-million-dollar inheritance.

I want her. I wanted her that night when she pissed me off by ruining an eight-thousand-dollar designer gown, her pleading gaze burned in my memory.

It will make things even more complicated, but I can't wait any longer. I turn her around and hold her to my chest, brushing my hands over her arms before I lift a strand of hair and press my lips against her neck. Her sigh causes a warm surge of arousal within me, excitement spiking. She goes with the movement easily, leaning back to give me more access, and I take everything she's offering.

"Is that acceptable?" she wonders breathlessly, and I have no idea what she's talking about. "I mean, before the wedding, that has to go against someone's idea of tradition."

"It will be fine if you don't tell anyone," I whisper, amused. I doubt she's seriously worried about that. If she is, I easily divert her mind when I cup her breasts in my hands, her nipples stiffening against my palms.

"Okay. I trust you." The last word comes out in a gasp as I pull up the skirt of her dress, to her waist, and let my hand slip between her thighs, fingers brushing lightly over the fabric of her panties. Then applying more pressure. Slow, but not too slow—neither of us is going to change our minds tonight. I sense her impatience which mirrors mine, but I'm not going to do this in the middle of the living room.

"Good," is all I say.

Stepping back, I turn her to me and kiss her again, steering her towards the double doors and into the bedroom. I finally get her all the way out of her dress which I toss on the floor, stopping to admire the black lace lingerie.

Reality, obligation, it all falls away for the moment, as my focus is on one thing, and one thing only. I get out of my blouse and pants as quickly as humanly possible, and then we are on the bed, her body warm and pliant under mine, my hands exploring every square inch on warm, soft skin.

She catches me by surprise when she's on top of me a moment later, straddling me. I indulge her for longer than I intended to, the contact too delightful to let it go. She's sweet, holding my face in her hands as she kisses me. When she straightens and removes her bra, I reach up to caress her breasts again, breathless from the desire in her gaze.

No, no one needs to know about this, and once we get it out of our systems, we'll never talk about it again. Until then...I pull her to me in a quick abrupt move, the need for control taking over, and Mia doesn't seem to mind. I push her panties aside, and back on top, finally finish what I started. My fingers meet her arousal, warm and liquid, the soft sounds escaping her lips nearly driving me to distraction—but I'm determined.

"You're right," she whispers. "I don't care what anyone thinks." Mia closes her eyes, her expression all bliss as she gives in to the inevitable.

My heart is still racing, my body thrumming with need, but that's one curiosity satisfied.

In the aftermath, I kiss her softly, easing her back down from the high. Everything about her, her taste, her touch, it's intoxicating, and dangerous. When was the last time I trembled in anticipation like this? I want to tell her to take her time, but apparently that's not Mia's intention. She loses no time kissing her way down my body, perhaps sensing my state.

It's too fast. I want to stop her, tell her not to rush but I don't. She's gentle, her mouth warm and soft against my collarbone, then exploring my breasts. I bit my lip but fail to keep in the sound, a I tense, muscles quivering when she moves further down. Her hands are on my thighs, gently parting them. She smiles at me, and for a second or so, I can't breathe. Then she leans in, and all the pieces fall into place. I slide my hands into her hair, and she indulges me, understanding what this means, what this, between us, is.

Ever since I met her, I haven't had the appetite to invite anyone else to this bedroom, and it had been some time since I had anyway, brief encounters with models usually taking place in hotels.

This isn't one of those encounters. It can't change everything, but for a few minutes I can pretend, the fantasy finally coming true. I give in to the rush of heat and lust, but I make it clear that I'll have the last word.

—ele—

Everything is near perfect, until she snuggles into my arms and holds on. Just a few minutes, I tell myself. She can't sleep here. I have work to do, I have to...Exhaustion and stress of the past weeks is creeping up on me too. Not an excuse, I know, but I close my eyes for a few seconds, only to wake up around four a.m. Mia is still in my bed, still cuddled up against me.

There is no actual danger—no one comes to these quarters unless invited. The issue lies elsewhere.

I might be cold according to some people, but I'm not that cold. Instead of kicking her out, I get out of bed and quietly get dressed. She'll find her way.

I head to my office where I brew myself a coffee before I turn on my computer and check my phone.

There's news, and it could be good or bad, depending on who you're asking.

Last night seems like a faraway dream, but at least I'll have that memory now. Nothing's going to happen in the next couple of hours or so, and I have time to work on my latest canvas.

Chapter Thirteen

Mia

I stretch languidly, smiling when the first sensation is the scent of Alessandra's perfume still on the pillow. For the first time in a long time, I feel exhausted in a good way, the way your body relaxes completely after sex that was every bit as amazing as I imagined it to be.

More to come.

Soon.

I hope.

I open my eyes, all of a sudden hit by the silence. It's still dark outside, no line of light from under the closed bathroom door either. Okay. By now I understand that Alessandra is near paranoid about boundaries, so it's not that surprising that she isn't here. Regardless of what I might have hoped. But it's too early, and I'm too tired to let doubts creep in. This was always meant to be, from the moment we met. It might not be the enduring romance I had hoped for, but it was...promising.

Heat rushes to my face and through my body as my mind wanders back to last night. I can't always read her, and she's frustrating me to no end, but I do feel safe with her.

I'm never sure what to make of all her promises, but this? My breath catches as I reminisce, my hands on her thighs, her body quivering against my mouth.

I learned that Alessandra is fine with reciprocity, and at the same time, she needs to make a point. I didn't, I don't mind. Part of me wants to recreate the memory, right now. I tell myself to be patient. She might come back before breakfast and...help me with that.

I pick up my phone from the nightstand, reality catching up with me somewhat. It's probably too early to call Lucy, but I feel guilty for not getting back to her right away when I learned what happened at the resort.

I didn't lie to Alessandra. Whatever retaliation she has in mind, I want to be a part of it, and I want Joey Moretti to know.

Alone in the dark, my mind goes in all kinds of directions. I could use this moment to find some more clues about my future wife, something that might help me in the future...While she and her siblings, and my parents didn't exactly show respect for my privacy when they packed up my apartment without asking me, I don't want to do the same.

To be the better person, maybe. And also, because this might be a test.

I still don't know all that much about her other that the intimacy we shared is something I want to repeat over and over again. And at the back of my mind, there's still that bit of sadness, because it's a lot, but it's still not enough.

Acknowledging that I won't get any more sleep, I get out of bed and head for the shower. Ten minutes later, my hair still wet, I walk downstairs. It's barely after five a.m., so the staff won't have arrived yet, but I can certainly make my own breakfast. I start with brewing coffee in the state-of-the-art machine, then inspect the fridge and pantry. I'm not surprised to find a multitude of choices. I cut some fresh fruit in a bowl, add yogurt, and choose a chocolate croissant to go with it. When the coffee is ready, I carry everything over to a sitting area by the window. After a first sip, I pick up my phone and text Lucy.

I'm so sorry. We'll talk soon but let me know if you need anything. I'm not sure how the message will be received, because the last time we met, I asked her for money.

From the window, I watch the darkness give way to the sunrise as I eat. It's much better, and less awkward to have a meal by myself if I'm not sitting at the giant dining table.

Lucy apparently has trouble sleeping as well, though for different reasons, I assume. Well, in a way they are all connected.

Some nice people swooped in and helped me secure the place, and they have been speeding up things with the insurance as well. Thank you, Mia. This was a shock, but we are handling it.

Now I feel even guiltier. If it wasn't for my connection to the resort, this would never have happened. I straighten in my chair, take a sip and wince as the hot coffee burns my throat.

No.

I might have been naïve about many things, but this is solely the fault of Joey and his clan. I'm aware that there has always been rivalry and competition, but this? What the hell were they thinking?

The irony. I could have the time of my life, if it wasn't all tied to mistakes and regrets, my parents', my own wishful thinking.

My musings are rudely interrupted when I hear yelling from the door, and then rapid footsteps.

"Where is she?" a male voice rages, and I recognize Joey Moretti.

I jump to my feet just in time before he barges into the room, flanked by two of his men. The premise is much different from the way it was at the bakery though.

Our own guards outnumber his. And the only way he could get inside is because someone let him. Alessandra's grandmother walks into the room after him, her anger matching his. Even though he stands more than a head taller, her posture is impressive, and the tone of her voice stops even him.

"I said we could talk. You come banging on our door at this time of the day, you play by the rules, Joey."

"What rules?" he laughs bitterly, as if he's the one who was wronged. His gaze falls on me, or maybe the table behind me, and he shakes his head. "Figures. Made yourself right at home, didn't you?"

"Show some respect," Nonna tells him coolly. "Remember that I helped your mother change your diapers."

He turns bright red, and I barely suppress surprised laughter. Though it's not that funny. People like us are friends until we aren't, though some arrangements last longer than others.

"What do you want?" I ask, feeling safe to step closer with a fierce elder and a bunch of armed guards in my corner. There's not going to be any shooting or attempted kidnapping today. Joey might be reckless, but he's not that stupid.

"I want to talk to the bitch who blew up my shipment."

"It's too early for your antics. And I didn't blow up anything." Alessandra has entered the room, and her cold-as-ice tone has everyone turn to her.

"Sure, you didn't do it yourself. You have your people for that."

"Be careful what you're suggesting, Joey."

Given the tense situation, the last thing I should be is turned on by her demeanor, but...whatever. "Mia, please wait for me upstairs."

I open my mouth to protest, but I catch her grandmother's slight nod and decide it's not the time to argue.

Joey's voice follows me all the way out of the room, "Pathetic, that's what you both are. You could have had a real marriage instead of this ridiculous imitation."

"That's enough. Do you have anything of importance to say? No? Then leave."

Out of sight, but still within earshot, I listen with a confusing mix of emotions. What if this escalates? And why does she still not want me by her side?

How can I change anything if everyone keeps underestimating me?

"You will pay for this," he threatens, and even from a safe distance, I flinch. Maybe he's that stupid after all. "You all will."

"You go anywhere near Mia, her family, or mine, and I promise you, you will regret it. You lost, Joey. Stay away from us, and you'll be fine. You can tell that to your father."

He bristles but turns away and storms out.

I hear the door slam, and I feel safe to go back into the room. Alessandra is standing in the middle of it, alone. Her face falls when she sees me.

"What are you still doing here? I told you to go upstairs."

"Do you remember anything I told you? That I need to know what I'm getting myself into?"

She just shakes her head and walks out on me, again.

My coffee has gone cold too, not that I care about breakfast any longer. But this time, I won't give up that easily.

I've seen another side to her.

I hurry after her.

"No. You're not walking away from me this time."

She stops, hesitates. Then she turns to me, her expression unreadable now.

"Come with me."

⁓⁓⁓

It's not a surprise that Alessandra doesn't mention Joey's stunt, or anything about the way she came undone under my lips and tongue last night. I allow myself a moment of pride but push the thought aside when she actually does have a surprise for me: She takes me to the headquarters of the Falcone company and introduces me to some of the staff I'll be working with now that their family is on the board of Leonard Logistics. She takes me to an office that's so new I can still smell the paint.

"You can start working from home, but you won't have to worry once you move into the office. The only reason a Moretti gets on any of our properties is because he's invited in, and I still have to have a word with Nonna about that. We have top notch security here and at home."

"So I've noticed. I had to climb out of the window, remember?"

Alessandra winces. "Don't do anything like that ever again. It was only a few days ago, so yes, I remember."

What about last night? It's on the tip of my tongue, and I might have blurted it out if it wasn't for the employees walking past us at that moment. I notice they greet Alessandra with something akin to polite reverence.

"Okay," I say instead. "Thank you." I search her gaze, trying to find...anything that connects her matter-of-fact, business-as-usual demeanor with the passionate lover I encountered less then twenty-four hours ago. Every single thought of it, every remembered sensation makes my knees go weak. Alessandra might not care about romance, or she might be pretending. She did ask Mom for the recipe after all. Also, she did much more than that...

"Are we going to talk about...?"

Alessandra shakes her head. "Not here."

She walks ahead of me down to the end of the corridor where she unlocks a door, and, making sure there's no witness around, pulls me inside. Seconds later, my back is against the wall, and her mouth on mine, hot, demanding. The moment is brief, almost unreal.

"You were saying?"

I don't need to hear more. She's been thinking about it as much as I have. Those kisses don't lie, even if we're still pretending with each other. Or she is. I don't know anymore.

"There's no need to talk, right?" Alessandra says, her hand on the door handle. "I can't give you the run-down of all our operations. If there's something you need to know, you will know. I can get you someone to help you brush up on self-defense if that makes you feel better. Let's just get this wedding over with, shall we?"

"Oh, sure, we shall," I mutter, straightening my clothes before I follow her out of the room. So, nothing much has changed in the grand scheme of things. I still can't get a straight answer out of her. I'm still mad at her even though seconds ago I was ready to let her do to me whatever she wanted to.

Meant to be? Or pathetic? Well, it looks like I have a job again. Why do I still feel so cheap?

Chapter Fourteen

Alessandra

I frown at the canvas, though the image coming to life is without a doubt beautiful, one of my best works. It's...inspired, which is a lot more than I can say about myself lately.

Nonna made a dangerous play, but Moretti has been laying low since the incident at the harbor, and I had a good, fruitful talk with our police contact. There was indeed a small explosion which led investigators to a major shipment of heroin hidden in containers carrying expensive floor tiles. Joey and his family will have enough on their plates explaining that to the authorities. It's of course payback for setting Lucy's resort on fire, but it also means we are getting a respite—and I can get married in peace. Still, I'm antsy, unsettled.

Mia, of course, it's all about her, the reason why we are at war with the Morettis now, my sleepless nights, the painting.

There is no easy way out of this with her. And apparently, I can't stop touching her, and she won't let go, won't stop giving me those gazes like she is convinced things can change in a heartbeat. They won't. I can't. I have a business to run, siblings to watch over, and secrets to keep. All of it despite being the target of Mia's anger and her longing...but now it's something I can't ignore.

A few more brushstrokes, and I have to change and get back downstairs. Before Bella and Enzo all but moved in, it was easier to steal away for a while, but I must keep up the pretense with them too.

I'm not sure what to do about Mia. A part of me already has accepted the inevitable.

I'm afraid someone's going to get hurt, but how can you stop when it's the pain you're addicted to?

—ele—

I spend some time at the office taking care of all the legitimate business. My family has always appreciated art, and sometimes, when I study reports and sign contracts, I take a trip down memory lane.

Trips we took with our parents, museum visits everywhere we went. I have memories of being entrusted with making sure Enzo or Bella didn't wander off, but even so, I had time to stand and stare in awe at giant canvasses and sculptures.

I showed talent early on and had specific tastes from a considerably young age. Compared to other families in the business, my parents were mildly conservative, and my siblings followed in their footsteps. I don't think either of them would appreciate it if the works of *Sela Andras*, gorgeous nudes, were attributed to me. There was someone, once, who knew about Sela. It ended badly. Now, those images stay behind closed doors, and for the most part, *SA* is nothing but a fictional persona.

Tough luck, I've spent most of my adult life making sure the less legal business transactions couldn't be traced back to us. Five hundred million dollars is a lot of money. A third of it still is.

We will all have a lot of options with this, especially given that we have an in with another company now.

Easy.

It should be.

But I have to keep an eye on Joey and his clan at the same time, keep an eye on my brother and sister who are too enthusiastic about the expected influx of money once I say I do, and...keep my boundaries in place, something I've done a rather shitty job of lately.

No one cares about my boundaries or feelings, and so I get ready for dinner after a quick shower, trying not to think of Mia, this afternoon, last night. Trying not to think of what would happen if she was here with me.

She's still mad, and at the same time eager, and there's a danger in that.

Once we're married, I need things to be stable, calm. The Morrettis will be put in their place, and they won't have much of a choice other than to accept this new reality.

We'll have considerable input in Leonard Logistics, and just maybe, there are parts of our business we could get rid of.

No one has ever called me naïve, but they certainly would if they could read my mind now.

I am tired.

～ele～

The sight of Mia at the dining table makes me a little less tired. I am thinking back to when she first arrived here, brooding in clothes that had no place in a formal context, hell-bent on running from the inevitable. Don't get me wrong, she is cute in those hoodies, but that moment she looked so young I wanted to back out. I don't mind the attention of a younger woman. I am not a predator looking to take advantage.

But Mia has many facets, all of which are dangerously tempting to me. Tonight, she's wearing a blouse with a plunging neckline, and a skirt, high heels to complete the outfit.

She's keeping me on my toes, and perhaps that's not a bad thing.

"We're good on the invitations, and I have most of the RSVPs," Bella declares, as if this were the most important issue we were dealing with. Well, it is an important issue. It matters who shows their face to celebrate this new alliance.

"Sounds like you got it under control," I acknowledge. "You got word from Kendall?"

"Yes. She and Robyn will be there as long as we come to the christening."

Mia looks up from her plate.

"I didn't know that they'd be there. Isn't it a bit risky?"

I give her a shrug in return. "Well, she's a distant cousin, and she still has a lot of friends in high places."

"She's also *persona non grata* to some people."

"People like the Morettis maybe, but neither my family nor yours has a problem with them."

True, Kendall is married to a former FBI agent who was still employed by the agency at the time of their wedding. Then again, we are friendly with the cops who busted one of the Moretti's lieutenants recently. Priorities matter. Appearances do. Given the power she still has, her presence is hardly negotiable, but Mia doesn't need to know all the details.

She shrugs and goes back to her meal, and for a few minutes, the atmosphere is calm, pensive almost.

The silence makes me drift.

"It will be fine," Bella assures her and everyone. "This will be the most secure wedding of all time. We have enough people to make sure of that."

I catch her gaze, and it's indeed reassuring to see my bubbly, giddy sister this calm and determined. I know my siblings' weaknesses, and their strengths. If Bella says it's fine, there's nothing to worry about. At least where the wedding day is concerned. My expression must have signaled something else, because Nonna says, "You heard her. Now, have you decided on a menu?"

The tone is a little lighter as Isabella shares her progress. Soon afterwards, she excuses herself, and Nonna says she's tired.

"But by all means, take your time. I assume you have a lot to talk about."

I swear she was this close to winking.

Nonna's not wrong though. There are things that Mia and I must address, and it's best done in private.

"Excuse me for a second?" I ask when we are alone. "I'll be right back."

She holds my gaze for a few heartbeats, seeming unsure how to react.

Truth be told it's easier for me to keep her wondering, even if for tonight, it won't last long. In my office, I print the necessary information and put it in an envelope. It might be risky, but I have to give her something, and I have to distract her from the happy ending she might still be imagining.

There is no such thing in our cycles, no matter what Nonna says. A good, solid partnership to keep the legacy going is the best we can all hope for.

Kendall, my distant cousin, marrying an FBI agent who then quit and will never have to testify against her? Smart.

Forging an alliance with the Leonards that not only guarantees us a substantial sliver of their business, but also saves us costs on transport, and allows us access to our grandfather's inheritance? Smart. That's all there is to it, being smarter than the others.

That's the story I tell myself when I return to the dining room where Mia hesitates between dessert choices.

"Take the ruby brownie," I say. "With an espresso."

"What, you want to keep me up all night?"

It's a good thing I don't blush, otherwise I probably would have at the blunt insinuation.

"Two espressos, one ruby brownie." I put the employee out of her misery, and she gives me a grateful smile.

"Coming right up," she promises before she heads back to the kitchen.

I put the envelope in front of Mia.

"What's this?"

"All the paperwork you need to access the account I opened for you."

Her eyes go wide.

"I thought...not before the wedding?"

"I changed my mind," I say. "I think you're smart enough," that again, "to understand what the Morettis are all about, and how far they will go. I don't expect you to play runaway bride."

And just in case, I add, "We might not be as ruthless as they are, but we don't like being embarrassed either. Keep that in mind, and we'll be fine."

She ponders this for a few moments, sighs.

"Sure," she finally agrees. The employee arrives with two espressos and the brownie on a plate. Mia waits until we're alone again before she continues. "Thank you. It's not like I need that money now, so I can just as well give it back to Lucy. I think she needs it more."

"You're welcome. And that sounds like a good idea. You'll have everything you need here, but you will have your own salary as well, so you won't have to worry about that."

"Okay."

I didn't expect the multiple emotions flickering over her beautiful features, and I'm struggling to decipher them all.

"I had no idea," she says, her tone disbelief with a hint of bitterness. "I mean, I knew Joey was an asshole, and that no one played 100% by the rules, but this is all...a lot," she finishes after not finding anything more fitting.

"I understand." I knew my role in the family as a child. She has been sheltered up to this moment.

"Do you? I didn't mean to be silly, or childish. I don't think it's too much to expect...Anyway. Can you really promise me that my parents will be safe? And that Lucy is?"

That part is easy.

"They're family now, and we treat them as such. Lucy will rebuild, and I've made arrangements for her to exhibit some of the artists we've contracted."

She shakes her head, a hint of amusement chasing the doubts and worries.

"Everything is transactional, right?"

"Isn't it? I return. "Now, are you going to finish that brownie?"

"Are you in a hurry?"

I steal a bite from her plate. It's delicious like everything that comes out of our kitchen.

"Maybe I do want to keep you up all night."

Mia, though prone to blushing, doesn't look away.

"I thought you'd never say it."

It's reckless, risky, but it looks like she's going to spend the night again.

I tell myself that no matter how tight security is, Mia's safety is priority, and she's safest when she's with me.

As if that's the only reason.

"Have you ever been painted?" I ask.

Chapter Fifteen

Mia

There's no chance I can get off this rollercoaster anytime soon. Because of my drastically changed circumstances, that's a given. The emotional part is another story.

It's reassuring to know that Mom and Dad, and Lucy, will be safe. My extended family, like Camilla, will be fine too. They have their own staff to take care of things.

The moment could be almost peaceful, but Alessandra tempting me with sweets and insinuations quickly takes any peace I could have here.

And I'm not opposed...

"Was painting a metaphor for something?" I wonder when we are in her bedroom, and her hands are all over me, my skirt hiked up to my waist. It doesn't really matter. Want is taking over every corner of my mind, every fiber of my body. Forget about my romantic dreams, I'll take this as long as I can get it.

For Alessandra, it's different, I assume. To her, establishing equilibrium means to keep power. It's not entirely equal, but I can't worry about that now.

I moan as her fingers slip past the waistband of my panties, knowing they will meet warm wetness. I can't pretend, and I won't try.

Alessandra doesn't linger, she turns me around and pushes me up against the wall. I'll start working soon, my family and friends are safe, who cares that our wedding is mostly a performance?

My questions dissolve into nothing when she pulls down my panties after giving the black lace an appreciating brush with her fingertips. I'm trembling. Speaking of...performance. She leans in, her hands firm on my thighs, and I barely have the chance to take a breath before her mouth is on me.

It's sort of spectacular how she takes control that way, and perhaps I knew it from the moment I saw her in the bar, and that is why I couldn't stop thinking about her.

That is why, despite this impossible situation, I allow myself to let go, and her, to take everything she wants.

It's messy, and quick, and I bite my lip in a failed effort to keep from making rather undignified sounds.

Aside from my panties pooled at my ankles, I'm still fully dressed.

Alessandra, however, is the opposite of a mess. She gets to her feet, a small content smile on her face as she straightens her clothes and pushes a strand of hair that escaped her neat bun, behind her ear.

"It's a good thing you had that espresso," she says, matter-of-factly.

We still haven't addressed painting. My curiosity can wait, other things can't.

I must have fallen asleep—and how could I not drift off, warm and relaxed in her embrace? She spooned me, holding on before I could even begin to talk about reciprocating, and I couldn't resist...but now she's gently shaking me awake, handing me a silky robe.

"Come with me," she says. Her tone is warm and sated, even though we haven't gotten to that part yet. In the short time since we've taken that step, I have learned that knowing what she does to me, is giving her satisfaction. I want to give her more, though the time of night is curious. 2:13 a.m. Whatever works.

"You have an office fantasy you'd like to act out? Should I get dressed?"

Alessandra laughs.

"No, this is fine. And we're not going to my office. I love what I do, but I don't need to do it twenty-four seven."

I'm curious. I've never seen her this excited—almost carefree. I am not naïve enough to think that having sex with me has put her in this mood.

We walk past an office area to yet another part of the mansion I haven't seen yet, and when she unlocks the massive wooden door, my jaw drops.

I always knew that the Falcones had secrets of their own, and that Alessandra was the most secretive of them, but I didn't expect this. Yes, I know she's an artist, and I have seen some of her work around the house, landscapes, still lifes. Even to my untrained eye, it's obvious that she has talent, but it is what it is—our aspirations have to take a backseat to our families' ambitions. At least that's what I thought, but as I walk silently along the giant canvasses, I realize that Alessandra Falcone doesn't compromise much.

The thought thrills and confuses me at the same time. If I'm not a compromise she has to make to get her hands on another company, for more money and power, what am I to her?

Did she tell the truth when she said she didn't know who I was, the night at the bar?

Behind these doors, Alessandra isn't painting trees, jugs, and pears. She's painting gorgeous nudes, the images so vivid I can't help a sliver of sensation coursing through my body. Especially given the fact that we just came from her bed.

I turn to her, and realize she's been watching me the whole time, her arms crossed over her chest. She's more at ease now than most of the time, and it's not hard to understand that within these four walls, she feels truly at home.

"Those are amazing." As if she doesn't know. This is the most important piece of the puzzle so far. And she chose to share it with me, even though she doesn't want love and romance in our marriage. It would take me a lifetime to figure her out.

"Thank you. How about we get started?"

"Get...what?" As if I hadn't been dumbfounded a few minutes ago. "Oh, no. I can't do that. Look at them. I'm not a model. I don't look like that."

She looks at me as if surprised by my ramblings. I'm not usually that self-conscious, but this is...particular. Everything about my current situation is. I'm barely catching up.

Alessandra reaches out to touch her fingers against my cheek. I can feel my skin warming under her fingers. Come to think of it, it's warm in this room, but that only makes sense if someone's naked in here most of the time.

"You are beautiful," she says, her tone warm and intimate and irresistible. "You don't believe me? Look."

She takes my hand and leads me over to a table with a few sketches scattered over it. I'm startled to realize they are all of me. Dressed. She didn't go that far.

As if reading my mind, Alessandra comments, "I didn't want to make anything up." She sounds amused.

"I don't know if I'm ready for this," I admit.

She embraces me from behind, the heat of her body melting away my inhibitions.

"Trust me. You've had a lot thrown at you in a matter of weeks, and you've been handling it all. This is easy."

I've listened closely to everything Alessandra has told me, and so far, she hasn't made any false promises. If she says it's easy, I'm inclined to believe her. What's the harm in this?

"Is this the equivalent of sending naked pictures?" I muse out loud, making her laugh.

"God, you're young," she says with so much affection it makes me want to kiss her. Go back to bed and show her it's mutual, has been for some time. Instead, I let the robe slide from my shoulders, completely naked under her gaze.

A smile spreads over her attractive features.

"Let's get you comfortable," she says, steering me to the loveseat at the back of the room.

I briefly wonder who lounged on this piece of furniture before, naked, the surge of jealousy not entirely unexpected.

"It's new," Alessandra informs me, as if reading my thoughts. I blush, her fingers cool and gentle against my cheek. Her touch is a little less sensual and more pragmatic as she positions my body to her liking. It's a bit awkward but thrilling at the same time.

How many people who aren't being paid for their secrecy have access to this place? Now, I am one of them.

—ꞇꞇ—

Alessandra amazes me, her ability to deeply and utterly focus, whether it's on business, art, or me. I never even imagined that someday, someone would paint me. Okay, so she's sketching for now, but there will be a painting at some point.

I have so many questions. The women in those other paint-ings—models. Did someone get close to her? I wonder what precautions were taken if they came here, and what they know, about Alessandra, and the Falcones in general.

They have kept the secret of the woman behind the name Sela Andras, though, and I imagine that both money and threats could have played a part.

The latter is not the only thing that's making me uncomfort-able. Alessandra lied to me. As time goes by, it becomes quite the strain to stay in the same position for such a long time. Add to that the fact that she woke me in the middle of the night for her artistic pursuits.

I can't be mad at her for it. I'm aware that it's important. For the first time, this is a secret that the two of us share, because I doubt it will ever leave this room.

I'm not sure how much time has passed when Alessandra declares the session over.

"When will we get back to it?" I ask, stretching and wincing at the sound of something cracking.

"Soon," she promises. "Let's go back now."

In her suite, she waits until I'm back under the covers, then disappears into the bathroom for a few minutes. I'm almost asleep when she returns, pulling away the covers.

"I think I'm kind of tired," I mumble, "but I could be tempt-ed."

"Silly," she says, and then her hands are roaming over my shoulders and back, delivering a firm massage that produces a kaleidoscope of sensations. Pleasure bordering on pain. It's so good, I'm content to just lie there and let her have her way with me. Even if she kind of insulted me.

"I usually give my models a gift card in addition to their payment," she says. "But since you'll be taking my last name…"

Has the last word been spoken on that already? I don't remember anyone asking me, but I'm too tired and caught up in the momentary bliss to argue.

Chapter Sixteen

Alessandra

Everything is finally coming together. I've wanted to paint her from the first moment I saw her, at the table with her friends. Something clearly weighed on her mind while everyone around her was laughing and chatting, oblivious.

Her eyes on me. Those inquisitive eyes. Mia will never stop asking questions, but I guess I found my ways to distract her. At least until the wedding. Once she's working full-time, we'll fall into a routine that hopefully doesn't include the Morettis in any way.

They've been silent, preparing a move, or coming to terms with the inevitable, it's hard to tell, but I don't trust them. I make a mental note to press Enzo about his girlfriend, the one that apparently has valuable insights regarding the family.

"You two seem like you've worked things out," Bella remarks, and I wonder why she came to breakfast—again.

Mia casts me a shy smile before she looks away.

"We're all on the same page here," I say. "Right? Is there any reason why we're seeing you this morning?"

Bella laughs at that. "I'm afraid you'll see me every morning for a little while. I am staying with you until the wedding. It's the best solution, so I can make sure everything goes smoothly. Mia's parents will arrive the night before the big event. If you have a minute, I can show you the accommodations I've made for guests from out of town."

Time has gotten away from me. The day of the big event is approaching fast.

What I get out of it...Another gorgeous painting, and a nice sum of money.

Mia gets...I catch her gaze on me, hopeful, before she averts it again. I hope she understands I took a big risk by taking her to the atelier. What it means. What it doesn't mean.

"I'll look it over, but I'm sure it will be fine."

She gives an exaggerated sigh. "Wow, this is big. I'm glad you finally see the kind of work I'm doing here." She can't hide the smile though. My sister has various tasks in the company, but she can't hide how much she's been enjoying this. Her dream business. Today, I feel like indulging her a bit. I'll call a meeting with Enzo later.

"We do appreciate it. So, are we ready?"

Her smile widens. Something inside is still resisting. The wedding day means exposure, and best efforts notwithstanding, a lot could go wrong. But I can't help it, a part of me is...looking forward to it? It's strange but true. We'll be among family, including many strong women who have always upheld traditions, and their respective businesses, some in visible ways, some in more subtle ways. I despise small talk, but I look forward to introducing Mia, and also, having the opportunity to talk to Kendall.

"We are," Bella confirms. "The venue is booked, everyone is assigned their seat, flowers, cakes, dresses and paperwork are all taken care of. Denise put me in touch with a make-up artist who has worked with Sabrina Russell and Molly Johnson, among others."

I can't help it, I shake my head with a laugh.

"Really, a Hollywood make-up artist? You don't trust me to put on some eyeliner and lipstick?"

"Exactly my point," she returns. "Don't worry. This will be the wedding of the decade, and it will send a clear message, to everyone who might think they can mess with us. And to the homophobic family members too," she adds. "I especially take pleasure in pissing them off. Don't try to deny it, you appreciate that too."

Fortunately, I'm not aware of that many, but she has a point. In family structures like ours, conventional, people can sometimes mistake bigotry for tradition. I don't think she needs an answer for that.

"I see you got it under control. Together with the hotel info, bring me the security plan. We'll look it over with Enzo later. Noon?"

"Only if it comes with lunch," Bella argues.

"You're eating right now."

She shrugs. "I'll be hungry then. You are infamous for calling meetings when normal, reasonable people eat or nap."

I take Mia's hand to get her attention. "And this, my dear, is what you'll have to put up with in the foreseeable future."

"Welcome to the family," Bella adds.

That air of feeling safe and relying on anyone other than myself is terrifying.

—— *ell* ——

I need Mia out of the way, so I've set her up in her office, so she can go over files and call a few people in her parents' firm who will consult with us on joint projects. I don't expect much to come of it today, but as long as she's occupied, it's all good.

Next, I call Enzo and tell him to bring Lilly to the meeting.

"I can't promise anything," he says. "She can't raise any suspicions."

"I got that part." Who is she anyway? "You haven't sent me her file yet. Please do it immediately."

"Yeah, sure," he mutters.

"Hey. The wedding is next week. We need to have everything in place."

"I'll send it right over. I'm sorry, Alessandra. I forgot."

I suppress a groan.

"Bring her and be on time."

We don't *forget* anything. It could cost people's lives. At least, true to his word, I get an email notification seconds after I end the call. I order more coffee and while I wait for it, I write an email to one of our contacts with the police. They'll provide someone who can show Mia the ropes.

I know that her parents made her take basic self-defense, but I doubt she has done much with it. It's not a bad idea to have someone teach her again. I hear back from my contact immediately, with a name and a time, which makes me smile.

It's good to have friends in the right places, especially when sometimes, they owe you.

On to Lilly.

I open the file and start to read. I don't need more than a few paragraphs to pick up my phone again, but this time, I only reach Enzo's voicemail.

I leave a message. *Whatever you do, bring her to the meeting.* He'll be able to tell from my tone that it's non-negotiable. How the hell could he not see this?

She might be somewhat friendly, considering that she gave us a heads-up the other time, but that's not guaranteed forever. I remember Mia's words—everything is transactional. She was right about that, and I'll have to make it clear to Lilly Whoever that we don't owe her for what she gave us. Make sure she doesn't get any ideas.

With a sigh, I check my messages, relieved to find my inbox empty for now. I'll deal with Enzo later.

At the company, trusted employees will have their eyes on Mia and inform me if someone so much as looks at her the wrong way.

It will be fine.

I keep telling myself that, but if it's true, why do I feel like I'm close to a panic attack?

I try to evoke the images and sensations from last night, just for a moment, so I can breathe again. That she has this effect on me is scary too.

It means I must do whatever I can to guard her, with my life, if necessary. I cannot lose her too. Something tells me that this time, I would never recover.

.

Chapter Seventeen

Mia

One step forward, two steps back, or so it feels. Who can blame me if I have trouble knowing what's real and what isn't, when Alessandra keeps drawing me into a sensual dream and then kicks me out the next day?

Okay, I'm being dramatic, but as I sit in my office, much aware of the presence of friendly guards, I can't help wondering how I should be feeling about all of it.

The painting. The out of this world sex.

Alessandra joking with Bella over breakfast, being openly affectionate, then sending me off to work, because she has some secret business to attend that I'm not privy to.

It's not that she lied about that too—she flat out told me that she'd never share all of it with me.

So, I'll just...Take what I can get? Is that the rational or pathetic way to go?

In any case, I have a real task today, and it feels refreshingly normal to sit at my desk and get some real work done. Most of the employees at Leonard Logistics know me from the time I worked there, and since I'm the owners' daughter, they don't ask me any questions beyond what's relevant for the respective projects.

The Falcones are going to use our infrastructure a lot more from now on, which means an increase to our bottom line, and an improvement to streamlining their operations. Everyone wins, or so it seems.

The morning goes by surprisingly fast, and it's almost 2 p.m. when my growling stomach reminds me that I skipped lunch. Alessandra showed me the break room when she first gave me a tour, so that's where I'm headed when one of the younger employees—not a guard—comes after me, looking self-conscious.

"Um...Ms. Leonard?"

We never got back to the subject of me taking her name either. At this point, trying to rebel and hold on to anything seems pointless, but I'll raise it with my fiancée as soon as possible. Tonight. Every once in a while, I manage to hold on to *her*.

"Yes, what's the matter...Jacob? Do you need me for anything?"

"Can I ask where you're going?"

I'm not the only one uncomfortable with some of the rules Alessandra has established in our life.

"I can assure you, I wasn't going far. Just to the break room."

"Ms. Falcone told me to let you know to order anything you'd like from the kitchen. The number is on your desk."

I suppress a sigh. He's serious? Is she?

"I can walk a few steps for a muffin. It's not a problem."

"They will bring you anything you like," he insists.

In a rather respectful distance, a woman stands with her back straight, observing the interaction. They still have guards all over the place. Not so much to keep me inside as to keep any possible foes outside, I know, but it's still irritating.

In any case, it's not Jacob's fault, or the woman's. Without another word, I return to my office.

I find the number for the kitchen and order a raspberry muffin with a white chocolate mocha. That's a lot of eating my emotions these days, but I suppose Denise will adjust the wedding dress if necessary. Or I'll find other ways to work off those extra calories.

I miss my work at Lucy's, the hours spent giving classes outside and hiking. To my surprise, I don't hate the coordinating job I've been given here at Falcone either, and, after my high-sugar indulgent break, I get back to it.

Alessandra sends me a text message to let me know she'll have someone pick me up at 5:00.

She'll have ID. Raven Winters.

All right, then.

The woman appears in front of my office door 5:00 p.m. sharp, startling me. She's dressed in black from head to toe, her expression impassive. I tell myself that if I'm not supposed to go to the breakroom, she certainly couldn't make it in here without passing some of the checkpoints.

I turn off my computer and grab my purse.

"Ms. Raven Winters? Could you show me..."

She hands me the document before I can finish the sentence.

"I assume you're my assigned driver for the ride home?" I ask, trying to make small talk.

A smile tugs at the corner of her mouth, but she doesn't engage.

Oh, whatever. I'm used to no one telling me anything. If my in-laws determine her safe, I decide that's what she is.

—ele—

I was sorely mistaken—and I'm going to be pretty sore later.

Winters isn't my driver. Alessandra kept her promise, and she's hired someone to teach me the basics again. She'll take me to the shooting range eventually, but today is for self-defense, and after the warm-up period, Raven doesn't pull any punches as she's testing me.

I might have been able to kick Joey in the shin, but despite the hiking and occasional yoga classes, I'm not in as good shape as I thought I was. Not that I can complain. I asked Alessandra for this, and she took care of it.

When it's finally over, and she hands me a bottle of water, I ask, "How long have you been working for Alessandra?"

"I'm not working for her," she returns. "I run my own firm. This is just a favor."

"Oh, really?"

She doesn't bite. "Yes. We'll pick up the day after tomorrow. Good job."

"Thanks...I guess." Being Alessandra's wife will be challenging on many more levels than I imagined. Strange to think that only a few weeks ago, I was completely oblivious. "I really am grateful. I guess you know we've had a situation."

"Yeah. Let's get you home."

I would have liked to take a shower first, but no one is inclined to take any risks.

It's as reassuring as it is terrifying.

A few days from now, I'll be married. About that, I pretty much feel the same.

Chapter Eighteen

Alessandra

I wait until we're all assembled in the room, blinds lowered, snacks provided, just so Bella doesn't complain. None of us will be going anywhere for a while, though I still keep an eye on my phone in case one of the security guards, or Raven, needs to contact me. It's quiet. Good. The next couple of hours or so will be tricky enough.

Lilly gives me a polite smile as she sits down next to Enzo. She drinks her coffee black.

"Lilly, I invited you here to thank you in person for the information you gave us last time. I'm sure my brother let you know it helped us a great deal. We appreciate it."

"You're welcome," she says, an air of caution about her as she sits up straighter.

"Now, it's not a secret that the Morettis are bad news, or that we have an important date coming up that they would love to ruin. I was wondering where exactly you stand on this...Special Agent Strickland."

Bella's eyes widen.

"What?" That was Enzo.

Lilly Crawford, that's the name she gave him, remains calm and collected. I like that about her.

"Don't worry, if he hasn't figured it out by now, Joey won't suspect anything. That leaves us."

"I'm not here to investigate you, or your brother."

But she would report any possible incriminating findings.

"Good. We don't want anything to happen at the wedding, or to you. So, we understand each other. Anything you learn about their plans to interfere, you come straight to us. In return, we'll make sure Joey never learns about your true identity."

"I guess that could work."

There's still caution, and a hint of anger, but she's too smart to let it show.

Enzo looks disappointed, still absorbing the news. I don't have the time or inclination to console him. How could he be this careless? It's like they all have forgotten. Moved on, moved past it.

I've had therapy. It didn't make me foolish.

"No, Lilly, I need you to confirm that it will work. If something goes wrong, your people won't want this on their conscience. You won't want that."

Laying it on a bit thick, I realize when she barely suppresses a smile. She also knows that the people in this room could make her disappear, if necessary. Not that I think it is necessary, but the impression won't harm. The air is thick with tension, until she says,

"Of course not. I'm surprised your fiancée isn't here. Enzo has told me about her. I wish you two all the best."

I'm not sure I buy that either, but she continues, "Never doubt that we have a goal in common. If Moretti doesn't get his hands on her or her family business, we both win."

Bella, ever the optimist, claps her hands.

"All right, now that we have that figured out, can someone get us more coffee?"

"I'm afraid I need to go," Lilly says. "He'll be expecting me in half an hour."

"Okay, you go. Keep us updated."

Enzo sees her to the door.

"Wow," Bella remarks. "How did you know?"

"It wasn't all that hard to figure out," I say, though perhaps I have a sixth sense for situations that could turn ugly at any moment. I wish I didn't have to learn the hard way.

Enzo comes back to the room and finds a bottle of cognac in the cabinet. He pours himself two fingers and slumps into a chair.

"Get it together," I snap at him. "You're married, for Christ's sake!"

"Well, that doesn't mean all that much today, does it," he returns in a scathing tone.

"You two, stop it. We avoided the worst, right? She's not going to serve us a warrant on the wedding day. Everything will go as planned."

I sure hope so. We have put the wheels in motion, and once that inheritance comes through, our family's standing will be unparalleled. Business, charities, investments, we will be near limitless.

Why then does it feel like everything is spiraling out of control?

I hope Mia is not too tired from her workout. I want to bring her back to the atelier.

———ɛɛɛ———

She isn't home yet when I return, and I take that time to sneak away to my favorite part of the house where I study last night's work. She might not be a professional model, but there's no doubt that she's beautiful, and I have enough confidence to know I have the skills to bring her beauty to life on the canvas.

Usually, being here for a little while helps me wind down from the demands of the day, but it's not working right now.

The brush is shaking in my hand, so I put it aside. That hasn't happened in a while. I can't believe Enzo has been this reckless...No wait, I absolutely can believe that. As usual, cleaning up the mess falls to me.

What would they do if I wasn't around for a few weeks—or months?

Mia put up considerable resistance when being called home to fulfill her duty to the family. And didn't she have a point? It appears that she was pretty happy working at the resort, the one that Lucy is still rebuilding.

I feel dizzy.

I wish I could just drop everything, and maybe Mia would even want to join me, go to Europe and visit museums, stay in hotels that are a piece of art themselves, see sculptures and paintings...Anything instead of this. I'm so tired of not only looking over my shoulder, but looking out for everyone else, all the time. Because they're so used to it.

Maybe they think it helps me, that I don't remember every day.

Maybe they even thought this whole idea of getting me married, of basically delivering Mia to me, would put an end to it. Perhaps I didn't feel the same about her as I do about Mia, this insane, undeniable attraction, but it was my responsibility to keep her safe all the same.

And I failed.

I miss her.

And just like that, it's getting harder to breathe again.

Chapter Nineteen

Mia

When I come home, I head straight to the shower, enjoying the feel of the hot water cascading over my sore muscles. As much as it challenged me, I'm glad to have the opportunity, and I look forward to working with Raven again.

Now, what I'm looking forward to is dinner. I get ready and head out to find Alessandra. I text her first and ask her if I should confer with the kitchen. No answer.

I saw her car in the parking garage, so I wonder if she's busy, or just doesn't want to talk to me. Either one could be true at any moment, but we didn't part on a bad note this morning, did we?

And she did remember my request. I wait another ten minutes, then twenty, and text again.

Everything okay?

She's not the only one who worries.

I contemplate asking Nonna, but I learn that she's going out for dinner tonight. When there's still no answer, I head straight for Alessandra's suite and try the handle.

"Alessandra? Are you there? It's Mia." I pause, feeling silly. "Did you get my messages? Please, open the door."

There's no answer, and I'm starting to freak out.

A security guard is heading my way, asking calmly, "What seems to be the problem, Ms. Leonard?"

"I need to see her. Now."

He looks doubtful, but after having to assert my position all afternoon, with the Falcones' employees, with Raven, I'm not backing down.

"Look, I know that you are not allowed past this door, but I'm going to be Mrs. Falcone. That means in a matter of days, you'll answer to me too. I need to check on Alessandra now, so get me the damn key."

I'm pretty sure he's not used to being talked to this way, but I'm long past caring.

"There is no key," he mumbles. "You activate it with your print. Hers, in that case. It won't work with yours."

I believe him, but to his utter surprise, and mine, my print unlocks the door. I head inside and close it behind me, frantically looking around. The bed is immaculately made. I go from the living quarters to the office and open the door to the atelier. It's dark in here, and I almost don't see her. When I do, I run over to her, crouch by her side.

"Alessandra! What's wrong?"

For a few seconds, I'm terrified. I'm so used to her being this cool, unshakeable person, with few exceptions, that seeing her like that throws me. She's sitting with her back against the wall, knees drawn up to her chest, tears streaking her face.

At first, I'm not even sure if she has noticed my presence, but her words leave no doubt.

"Go, Mia. I'm fine."

"You don't look fine. Tell me what happened, please? Let's get you up from the floor at least."

"I told you to leave," she snaps. How can she expect that of me after those intimate moments we have shared—in her bed, and here, in this room?

"I'm not going to, and I'll apologize later, but I need you to get up, get warm and come to dinner with me. Let's order some pizza, or any comfort food you'd like." I pause, wondering if I'm in over my head. I still know so little about the woman I am going to marry, though parts of the picture are becoming clearer. "Please? I swear I'm not going to ask any more questions. I just want us to have dinner."

Realizing that I'm not giving in, she accepts my hand and gets to her feet.

"I'm going to take a shower," she mumbles and pushes past me.

I follow her back into the bedroom where I sit in a chair. Alessandra raises an eyebrow, but doesn't comment, just picks out some clothes and heads for the shower.

Her shield will be back in place, no doubt, when she returns. For once, I'm okay with it if that's what she needs. It's somewhat reassuring.

I'm aware that it was hard for her to let me see her like that, but I'm glad that I did. I need to know what I'm in for if there's anything I can help her with. Even if I can't, I just want to be there.

For better or worse. I shake my head at myself, but this is not about my starry-eyed notions of marriage. We have to present a united front.

I get it now. I will do my part.

~ele~

I was right. Alessandra steps out of the bathroom, fully dressed, her hair in a ponytail.

"You're still up for pizza?" she asks. "I let the kitchen know. A Chianti would go well with that. How was your day?"

"Yes, and good." Of course, we're not going to order in like ordinary people. No doubt about it, the Falcones are in a different league, but for once, I let it slide. "Raven was a bit of a surprise, but I think we'll work well together."

"Oh, I know you will. She called me."

"Alessandra..." I have to try, but I soon realize I won't be getting anywhere tonight.

"I'm fine. Let it go," she says, sounding pained.

"You don't have to be embarrassed..." I didn't expect the flash of anger in her expression. "...or worried. About anything. I swear I won't tell anyone."

"That's good. Otherwise, I'd have to kill you."

"What?" I squeak.

"It was a joke."

"Not a good one." I'm aware of how tired she is. "All right, let's have dinner. No one will suspect anything. I might have yelled at the guard earlier, but they're used to my moods...Why does my print work for this lock?"

"Clearly, it shouldn't," she mutters.

Pizza and wine still count for comfort food, even if it comes from the luxury kitchen which is part of the mansion's accommodations. I can forget about that for a moment, but it's hard to forget about what I witnessed. I want to help. I don't know how. What I do know is that she told me in no uncertain terms to leave it alone, and for now, I have no choice.

Is Nonna aware of what's going on? Is everyone but me?

"You can stop speculating," she says. "I had a moment. It's over. We have other things we need to focus on."

I feel busted. I take a bite of pizza first, thinking that if this arrangement with Raven is a regular thing, I'll be fine.

"You're right. But if there's anything you'd like to talk about..." I get inexplicably emotional. I always thought it mattered, communication in a relationship, but I guess that's still not what we have.

Even Mom and Dad decided they'd go along with the Falcones' offer before consulting me. They do and decide everything together.

Well, part of it is what got me into this mess, but no one could predict how I'd feel about her.

"I just want you to know you can."

"I appreciate it. But don't worry. It's been a long day, that's all."

I don't ask. I know it would likely be futile. However, I watch her closely, relieved that she seems to be feeling better.

I'll have to be more subtle, listen for hints between the lines.

"Would you like to work some more on the painting later?" I ask. It's not code for anything. I'm curious about the final result, and for some reason, in that room, I feel closer to her.

Perhaps that could be good for both of us.

"If you're up to it," she says, her tone even, but there's a hint of hope to it.

"Absolutely."

Chapter Twenty

Alessandra

By the time the wedding day comes around, we have fallen into a rather comfortable routine. It's a relief that Mia doesn't ask any more questions.

I keep her busy.

At work, she's finding her footing, and Raven is happy with her progress. Good. The more she focuses on the matters at hand, and the less on me as a mystery she feels needs solving, the better this marriage will work.

And whenever we find the time, Mia strips naked to pose for me, and I reward her patience with sensual massages, among other things.

Lucy got her money back, and then some, as an anonymous donor is helping with the rebuilding costs. It's really not that much, given the amount of money that will flow towards our accounts on the wedding day.

We haven't heard back from Lilly. Enzo is brooding whenever I see him, but he keeps assuring me that all is quiet.

So far so good.

Is it?

I'm aware of Nonna giving me pensive glances as well. She senses something, though I'm pretty sure that Mia didn't talk to her.

The day before the wedding I leave my office early and head home. I've made sure that Mia will be stuck in meetings until later in the evening, Nonna and Bella are out finishing up last minute errands, and Enzo is holding down the fort.

In the atelier, I stall, leafing through the sketches I made of Mia, before I knew who she was, and after I got to...discover her.

I mix myself a drink, a quick Old Fashioned, and sip on it before I finally take the key out of the desk drawer and go to the back of the atelier, unlocking the door that has stayed close since I stored the canvases in there.

I take them out one by one, my breath catching in my throat. I deleted the photos from my phone, all of them, trying my best to erase that period from my life. If it never happened, neither did the grief, and I never have to fear it could happen all over again.

Who was I kidding?

Keeping Mia at arm's length every step of the way, I'm doing it even now. Even before that, agreeing to this arrangement. I see the logic in it, truth be told, because it is a lot of money. I believe it shouldn't just be lying around, and well, I was the only one not yet married.

But what if I want more out of it?

Reflected in those paintings, I see my limitations and short-comings, angry because I nearly cry again. It would have been so easy. I was on the verge of blurting out the whole sad story, let her...What, hold me?

She does, at night sometimes, snuggling up and sneaking an arm around my waist when she thinks I'm asleep. I soak it all up, never tell her in the morning. How sick is that?

Again, I look at the woman on the canvas. She's smiling, oblivious to the tragedy about to unfold.

We don't talk about how everyone knows who was responsible for the shooting that day. The person in question was dealt with swiftly, and we moved on with our lives.

We had no proof that Moretti had a hand in it, though it wouldn't surprise me.

The lesson it taught me has haunted me ever since, and that's why I can't give in to Mia's fantasies of romance and a happily ever after. It doesn't exist.

If it hurt this much to lose someone I never even loved, I don't want to love.

And so far, I've done okay.

Getting married will make no difference, though I'm strangely excited about it all.

"Goodbye," I whisper before I put away the canvasses and lock the door again.

I'll be okay. I just needed a reminder.

Chapter Twenty-One

Mia

I am giddy, overwhelmed with emotion and sensation. It's nearly two a.m., the day before the big day, and we haven't slept yet. Alessandra made good progress on the painting. To my surprise, she let me see it this time.

It's not done yet but seeing myself through her eyes amazes me. I think I'm okay most of the time, better with a bit of deliberate make-up and hairdo, but most of the time, I don't dwell on it.

But that painting...It is beautiful. It makes me blush to look at it, because the woman in it portrays all the confidence and serenity of someone comfortable in her own skin, so much more than I am on most days. I am when we are together, like tonight, when a sensual massage blurred into something deeper, inevitable. I'm still catching my breath, lying on my stomach as her hand gently caresses my back.

Alessandra kept her word too. Lucy sent me photos of the progress at the construction site, and she told me about an anonymous donor. When I asked her about it, Alessandra shrugged, but I can read her a little now. I know where that money came from, but it's fine if no one else knows.

"We should be sleeping," I say with a yawn.

"Then stop tempting me." Her tone is so matter of fact, I can't help laughing.

"So it's all my fault, huh?"

"Oh, it is, but it's quite pleasant."

Alessandra places a kiss at the center of my back, making me gasp.

"See?"

She might have a point. Who cares if we're tired at the wedding? It's all fake anyway. This isn't.

Given everything that has happened, it's a surprise that I have no sense of foreboding. I can't tap into that feeling of anger and betrayal either, at least not for the moment, because I've gotten so used to living in this house and working in the family business. Two families, two businesses that will be joined together.

No going back.

Relatives, mine and the Falcones', have arrived from out of town, but I won't see most of them until later when the wedding is being officiated. The vast backyard has been decorated for the occasion, and we'll be standing right inside the white gazebo surrounded by purple flowers.

Out of the window, I can see more preparations in progress, and I realize I can barely breathe.

I'm getting married.

To an aloof, gorgeous woman who sees this wedding as a transaction, except when we dare to venture outside the boundaries. Will it be enough? Can I live with the compromise?

We shall see. I realize that my condition has less to do with any worries, and more with the fact that I'm excited out of my mind.

I barely managed a cup of coffee and a piece of toast this morning while Camilla and Sadie, who snuck into the room, have already started on the champagne. Nonna is sitting in an armchair by the window, her expression...proud? I feel like that's more than I deserve, but it's making me emotional. She gets to her feet when there's a knock on the door, preceding Mom and Dad.

After a warm greeting, she says, "I'm going to check on my granddaughter now. I'll see you all later."

She squeezes my shoulder gently, and I'm reminded of how she took on Joey Moretti.

I don't have to worry, not about him at least. I'm surrounded by people who will protect me. I know that now.

And thanks to Raven Winters, I can protect myself as well.

"How are you feeling, Mia?" Mom asks, so I smile, and then I have to blink, because I don't want to cry in front of them.

"Okay, I guess," I say, even though that's an understatement. Of course, I can't share that mind-blowing sex with my future wife has eased my mind regarding a painfully unromantic arrangement...Not that anyone could guess.

The backyard looks beautiful, all that splendor and luxury easily hiding the reality of it all. What is that anyway, at this point?

Everyone is excited, happy.

For us. A few of them, for themselves too.

This might not be a traditional wedding as to everyone's interpretation, since we couldn't have it in a church, but I don't think anyone cares. It's a celebration.

I feel celebratory.

"It will be okay," she says and hugs me close.

"Yes, Mom. I know."

I almost gave myself away, but I can't tell her something I haven't quite acknowledged myself yet.

There will be time, after Alessandra and I make it official.

After she finishes that painting.

We still have many conversations ahead, but today is not the day for them.

Today, we will say "I do."

Chapter Twenty-Two

Alessandra

I'm caught between a feeling of foreboding and anticipation. I don't know, maybe the two are the same? No, that's silly, we took every possible precaution. Moretti might be a sore loser, but brooding is all he's doing for now.

The nervous fluttering of my stomach doesn't come from a premonition. I can handle a crisis if I have to, but I never expected this marriage to be more than a business deal, and I expected my future wife to be on board with that.

Who am I kidding? I'm in over my head, and I stopped caring. Once I took Mia to the atelier, once she said yes to this kind of scrutiny, it was done.

I'm enthralled.

I'm amazed how much she has changed in such a short time, taking initiative at work, in her new position, and at home, in the bedroom. She's become a...suitable partner. Protecting her isn't only to keep the promise we made to her parents, or for that obscene amount of money we stand to get.

It's become a need, and however it makes me feel, it's not going away.

Nonna came to see me before the ceremony. She didn't say much, just hugged me close and assured me we were doing the right thing. If it hadn't been her, I might have been a tad irritated—I know we are doing the right thing. I would have never agreed to this plan if I thought it wasn't worth it. Was there ever a question?

Fast forward to the unreal moment of me, standing at the front of the gazebo with the officiant. I know the woman, another artist, and the niece of a *capo* from a family we've done business with before. My gaze falls on Nonna sitting in the first row, happiness written all over her face. I'm sure she misses her husband whom she married for love, and who played this trick on all of us. Well, it works out in the end. For me and my siblings. For Mia.

All the seats have been filled. Enzo, Bella, Uncle Paolo, and various more distant relatives. I spot Kendall and Robyn. Mia's family, her mother Flavia who has an air of gratitude about her. I can imagine it's a weight off their shoulders to have the Morettis out of their business.

Lucy, Mia's cousin Camilla and their friend Sadie. The latter two look teary-eyed, but it might be the champagne that has been going around since this morning.

The music starts, and along with it, the most traditional and archaic element of this day, the giving away part.

Vincente is wearing a joyful smile as he leads his daughter along the pathway between the rows of chairs, but I barely pay attention. Sarcasm eludes me when I take in Mia walking next to her father, her head held up high. Arranged marriage or not, she will always be her own woman, and I love that about her. My throat goes tight for a heartbeat, my vision blurring for no good reason. Not now. It's not a good time for revelations when we have to get through the ceremony.

I can't ignore the facts though. Her eyes meet mine and she smiles. I can't help smiling in return, because I know after this, we'll return to the atelier, and sooner or later, we'll find time for a more private, intimate celebration of this union.

Ironic how even before today, Mia became my muse, something I couldn't find from changing models who graced my canvasses and my bed. They came and went. Mia is going to be my wife, ideally...Till death do us part. I ignore the shiver skittering down my spine, too mesmerized by the sight of her.

Her dress is made with intricate details, and she wears it proudly like the generations of women before her. She might have had doubts, but it fits her like a glove, and she, in this dress, fits into this day, with me.

I have to admit Bella and Denise did a great job helping me find one that doesn't clash, and the Hollywood renowned make-up artist Bella hired was definitely worth the money.

We will send a message for sure, to the Morettis, and to any relative who clings to antiquated views. This is the modern version of a connected family. We are consolidating power in, I'd like to say, an unprecedented way, but perhaps Kendall did something similar when she married Robyn. We're not going back.

Mia's hands are cold, warming in mine when we speak our vows. They are fairly short and to the point, as expected by everyone under the circumstances.

She's already mine, but that's a private matter between the two of us.

We exchange a smile, more co-conspirators than lovers or wives at this moment, and the officiant declares that we can kiss our respective bride.

We lean in at the same time and meet in the middle. I can hear the cheers, mostly but not exclusively from the younger guests, and assume there are a few stern looks as well. I don't care.

Now, we will all get what we want, and so much more money is going to flow into my passion work, and the legitimate parts of the business. As long as Enzo and Bella stay reasonable, we're golden.

Mia holds me in a tight embrace, almost too close, but I can indulge her for a bit.

It's a glorious day.

⁓eɛe⁓

She doesn't move from my side, and neither do the multiple guests who congratulate us and push glasses with champagne on us. I manage to resist for the most part, smile and thank them.

Mia doesn't resist all that much now that the most official part is over. I can't ignore the look she's giving me, so full of...a kind of admiration I'm not sure I deserve.

Another conversation for another day.

But there's something I do need to take care of, and it can't wait much longer.

I meet Bella and Enzo in the office where he immediately goes for the whiskey. For once, I don't mind. It's a day of celebrations, or at least, if everything went according to plan. This is the moment to find out.

Bella is holding a colorful cocktail, but I know there's no alcohol in it. After that one glass of champagne, she sticks to mocktails which makes sense given her responsibilities today.

"How much longer is this going to take?" he asks.

I'm not going to tell them, but I'm a bit excited myself. We have been comfortable all our lives, aware of our privilege, but this is still a game changer. This will elevate us to the pantheon of connected families, leaving crooks like the Morettis far, far behind. It couldn't come at a better moment.

This is for Giorgia, for closure.

And it's for Mia, for the future.

For our families.

A few clicks later, I'm in the account, and I turn the screen so Enzo and Bella can see the numbers. I suppress a smile when I see both their jaws dropping slightly.

"Come on, you didn't think this was a joke? May I remind you this was the whole point?"

The estate lawyer our grandfather had hired would have a lot to explain if the balance wasn't what it is.

"Damn right," Enzo agrees, clinking his glass against mine. "To us. No one can stop us now."

Technically that's right. In reality...

"Don't forget it's better to be a bit more subtle about it," I warn him and Bella snorts. Point taken. Subtle isn't our brother's strongest suit. "No sudden moves, and if you want to take that FBI agent on a luxury vacation, you better wait a few weeks."

"She's a friend. Married," he mumbles, amused.

As if that has ever stopped him.

"It could be a good investment though."

I share a look with Bella who shrugs.

"Whatever you do, don't risk too much exposure. In the coming weeks, we'll talk about new investments some more. There's a lot of opportunity for new and existing real estate, new galleries, ateliers...No need to spend it on a beach trip yet."

I know what his slightly patronizing expression means.

"Expanding into these areas means we can slow down on others," I say. "You know this was always the plan."

"Was it though? I understand you got cold feet after Giorgia—"

"She was murdered," I interrupt him sharply. "That has nothing to do with what we're discussing here. We all need to make smart moves."

"We need to pay the bills too," he returns. "But like you said, we have time to talk about it. The most important part is done. Now enjoy your wedding day."

I don't say it out loud, but I would enjoy it more if, once in a while, I didn't need to babysit him.

Bella's gaze is pensive. I know that she, too, has big dreams regarding this money. Bigger than you can realize in a few hours, or even days.

"All I'm asking is take the time to consider your next steps, and make sure it's in line with all our business interests. That's what Mom and Dad would have wanted us to do."

They don't argue with that, not so much because I'm right, but because they can't prove otherwise—and it is my wedding day after all.

I log out of the account, close the site and get to my feet.

"Congratulations to us. We'll come back to this at the end of next week—if there's anything before that needs to be addressed, let me know. I'm going to find my wife now."

"I still think you should have taken a few days for a honeymoon," Bella muses. "We can handle things here."

This is where I put my foot down. We will travel for business eventually, but a honeymoon would signify all the things this marriage can't be. I hate that I feel a pang of regret.

Mia, with all her hopes and ideals about marriage, hasn't said anything, and I wonder if she and Bella talked about it.

She might have wanted it, and I can't help thinking it would be nice to get away from it all for a little while.

There is no time. She will understand. We will have our escape right here at home.

That escape won't be for another few hours, as there will be a dinner and a cake to cut into...I'm exhausted already. This is different from calling the shots in the boardroom. It's a big, loud, happy party.

I think it's time to find Mia and take her aside for a moment, see where her head is at.

Earlier, she was with Camilla, Lucy, and Sadie, but when I return, I see the three women standing together near the bar, chatting. When I come closer, I hear Lucy talking about how the rebuilding of her resort is going, and that it will be more beautiful than ever. Vincente and Flavio are talking to Uncle Paolo, Nonna is sitting with one of my aunts.

How's that for foreboding? I ignore the sentiment and approach Mia's friends.

"Do you know where Mia is?"

Of the three of them, only Lucy looks concerned. "She was going to find you. You didn't see her?"

Sadie laughs. "I'm not surprised, this property is huge! It's beautiful, by the way. But the size is insane. I was afraid I'd get lost looking for the bathroom."

"That's why there are signs," I answer mildly, my tone not revealing my rapidly beating heart. "So, she went inside?"

"Yes, about twenty minutes ago."

Damn it. A lot can happen in twenty minutes. I don't even care if I'm paranoid. I'm heading right back to the house and up the stairs. Mia isn't in my suite, or hers, or in the atelier. Or anywhere in the house. I text her.

Call me when you get this. Right away.

I send messages to Bella and Raven as well, more unsettled with each second. We were as careful as we possibly could be. Security everywhere. Vetted personnel, vetted guests.

I always assumed Joey would want to try something, but all of those measures were supposed to keep him far away. Besides, he must know that there are very few people he can count on by now, as everyone is aware of shifting alliances.

Where is Mia?

I can't lose her, and not just because I couldn't live with the repeated failure.

I can't lose her because I'm deeply and hopelessly in love with her.

How's that for a revelation?

Chapter Twenty-Three

Mia

I know that there are still many secrets between us, like the reason why she was crying the other day, business ventures between her and her siblings...I'm all right with going slow, but I'm not all right with her leaving me alone on this day.

If it's something that important, I should be privy to it, shouldn't I?

I can't fool myself. It wasn't my choice at first to be a part of all this, but I'm in it now. This is my home. I work as a liaison between our families' companies, which will eventually become one.

There are so many things I understand now...What Alessandra is willing, and able to give, and what I'll never get from her. And what we have is so much more than I ever could have imagined.

I love her. If need be, enough for both of us. I think it's about time she knew that if she doesn't already. The moment I put on this dress, walk down to meet her, I couldn't deny the obvious, and I'm no longer afraid...

At least that's what I think, until in the empty hallway, a voice from behind orders,

"Don't move."

It's not the person I expected, but that doesn't mean anything. Families like ours move with the times, lesbian arranged weddings and all, so it wouldn't be surprising if some of the Morettis' minions were women.

I raise my hands, my heart starting to race as I slowly turn.

"I said don't move."

The sound of a gun's safety being released is unmistakable, and I do as she tells me.

Now what?

"Whatever you want, can't it wait? As you can see, this is kind of an important day for me."

If I can get close enough, and if I can make her comfortable enough so she puts away the gun, I could maybe put one of those moves Raven taught me, to good use? It's not likely, as she certainly didn't have three or four glasses of champagne, but I'd give it a try.

"Well, it's important for everyone. I don't want to hurt you..."

I snort.

"We just need you out of the way for a few hours, that's all. Now, let's go, Mia."

I feel sick. What's going to happen in those hours? Is Joey planning to blow up the place?

I spin around, seeing that she's dressed in all black, wearing a mask, an ordinary minion fashion statement.

"Don't try anything, and everyone will be fine," she warns.

I try anyway, but the dress doesn't allow much movement, and the sting of a needle ends the argument.

When I come to in a non-descript room, an empty office somewhere in a commercial building, I have a headache, and my state of mind wavers between strong annoyance and sheer panic. Back and forth. And again. I'm getting so dizzy just from the emotional roller coaster, I might throw up.

To my relief, my dress, the one that generations after me are supposed to wear, is still intact. So am I, mostly. The woman didn't bother to tie me up, and I carefully move into a sitting position.

I wish Joey would show his face so I could give him a piece of my mind.

Who else could be behind this?

There's no clock in the room, and eventually, my heartbeat calms down. There are no sounds, nothing, and I'm almost getting bored, starting to drift off, so I get to my feet and examine my surroundings more closely, not that there's much to see. The view from the window is of a group of unfamiliar buildings. As I walk around, my mind starts to clear.

Whoever took me, and I'm still convinced that their name is Moretti, wants to keep me off balance. I don't trust that they don't want me, or anyone at the wedding party, harm, most of all Alessandra.

I think of the harm that could come to her or the other guests, the damage to the beautiful home...and her life, should the wrong people find out about her secret. This family would sure be petty about Sela Andras' paintings, and I don't know how her own would handle them.

The door is locked, there is no other exit, and the window doesn't open.

Looks like I'm stuck here for the time being.

My phone is gone.

I'm not going to cry and give him that satisfaction. When I look Moretti in the eye, my carefully applied mascara will be intact too.

Chapter Twenty-Four

Alessandra

Everyone has gotten back to me, except for the most important person: Mia.

"How the hell is it possible that none of you, who planned this day to the last detail, have any idea where she is?"

Raven flinches, and Bella does too. They know that apologies won't cut it, and they certainly won't get any from me until Mia is home safe and sound. It might take a while. Someone messed with the security cameras in vast areas of the house. At least we can determine which way out they took, but there's no sign of anything helpful, no tire tracks, nothing. She just vanished.

"Enzo, get your girlfriend in here. Now."

"She's not my—I'm on it," he changes course when I glare at him. Downstairs, none of the guests have learned of the emergency yet, and if it's up to me, they never will.

But it's not up to me, and we have no lead.

Soon, we will have to involve police sources, and then we can't hide what happened any longer.

If he hurts her, Moretti is a dead man.

I have no qualms going there, no matter who might be a witness.

——ℓℓ——

Lilly texts Enzo that she can't leave, so he and I will go over to talk to Moretti directly. I want to stay friendly with her, but at this point, I'm more concerned about Mia's life than about her cover.

I have changed out of my dress into more suitable attire, nothing I can do about my make-up now. I'm brimming with nervous energy and rage, becoming aware of it when Enzo keeps giving me strange sideways glances. I force myself to calm my breathing.

If Moretti wants to play games, he has no idea what he is in for. We can destroy him now. Come to think of it, why wait?

We don't even make it all the way to the front door. His goons greet us at the gate as we get out of the car.

"Hey, Vittorio, open the damn gate," Enzo yells. "We know what Joey did."

They look impassive.

"Doesn't he have the guts to come out here?"

"We are wasting our time," I say, keeping my tone cool. "Courage has never been Mr. Moretti's strong suit. If he doesn't want to talk to us, well, we have other means."

I can see the discomfort in their faces, and one of them uses a mike to speak to someone in the house.

"Five minutes," he warns. "Then you leave."

Enzo crosses his arms over his chest. "We'll see about that."

I admit I am surprised when Joey shows up at the gate a couple of minutes later.

"Hey, whatever you're selling, I'm not buying," he jokes. "I can get a better product anywhere. Alessandra. You already got tired of your bride, so you came here to bother me?"

"Cut the crap and tell me where she is."

Something about my tone has alerted one of the goons. I can see his hand going to his gun. I trust myself to be faster, but I can't believe Joey is that stupid. Is he?

"What?" He laughs. "That's what you came here for? I have no idea where she is. Did she run? That's hilarious."

"The only time she ran was to get away from you. And you burned down her friend's business," I remind him.

"Ah, let's not make petty accusations. I am enjoying my afternoon, and I can assure you that Mia is far from my mind. Honestly...She's a brat. You deal with her."

Sometime soon I'll teach him what happens to people who insult my family, my wife.

"I don't think you completely understand your situation. The police have been closing in on some of your partners. I could make a couple of calls and get a search warrant for your warehouses within the hour. You know that, Joey."

His expression becomes guarded.

"Really? You don't want to do that, Alessandra. I have no interest in her, and I have no fucking clue where she is hiding. But if you want war, you can have it. We all have skeletons in our closets, and I know more than you think about yours, and those of your friends."

For a split-second, he startles me, but there's no way he can know about Sela Andras and the nude paintings. Unless one of the models broke the NDA. It's not important right now, and besides, I know he's lying.

"Friends."

Everyone knows I keep to myself. Enzo and Bella have their areas of expertise, but I don't involve them in everything, let alone...

"Don't try to deny it. I know you're tight with Kendall Mancini."

"Tight? She's a distant cousin."

"And that Caruso woman. I'm warning you, think carefully about how far you want to take your little feminist revolution."

"You're not making any sense. I don't have time for your bullshit."

I hate to leave empty-handed, but at the moment, I have no choice. We'll have to set something in motion.

After that...Who knows?

If this wasn't so damn serious, I'd be amused he thinks that I'm planning something with these women—while participating in an arranged marriage no less. Kendall has her own turf, and she's smart enough to stay in her lane. Caruso is a name that gets dropped every once in a while, but I have no reason to see her as a friend or foe.

Who cares about Joey's delusions?

I need to find Mia. Now.

———

"I can't believe this happened! You were supposed to protect her!"

Each of Flavia's words feels like a blow, and I deserve every single one of them. We managed to keep most of the guests oblivious, but Nonna caught us sneaking back in, and she insisted that Mia's parents needed to know.

Not that there's much we can tell them. Joey lies whenever he opens his mouth, but strangely enough, he sounded sincere when he said he doesn't know about Mia's whereabouts. I brush off the shadow of doubt. He's lied so many times, probably even he can't tell the difference anymore.

We must react, one way or another, and so our police sources receive another tip. This is just the beginning—it won't end the Morettis altogether, just rattle them a bit when a few of their goons are taken out. Traffic violations, theft, domestic violence, assault, we are keep an eye on the people they associate with for a reason.

They won't talk to the authorities, too scared of Moretti senior, but it will shake something loose.

Meanwhile, the fear is tearing me apart. I can't let that show either.

"We are going to find her," I promise, wishing I had the luxury of having a breakdown.

Where is she?

Chapter Twenty-Five

Mia

Whoever has locked me in here, obviously has lots of time. I only have the daylight to gauge, but I'm certain that at least a couple of hours have passed. No one has come to see me.

I decide I don't have that much time to waste. It's difficult, but I try to remove all the worries about possible scenarios from my mind and go back to the moves Raven has taught me.

We even went back to the shooting range once where we realized that while I'm a bit rusty, I'm still decent—not that it's going to help me now. I can only rely on myself. The element of surprise.

I can't fall asleep, though the temptation to just lie down on the carpeted floor is strong.

No.

Alessandra expects better of me.

I expect better of me.

It's my wedding day, and I'll do whatever it takes to get back home, to her.

Where I belong. My eyes well up at the thought. I want to wipe a hand across my face, then think twice and dab lightly under my eyes.

No crying until we can cut that cake. No one is getting hurt today. I might be drugged, or naïve, but I don't care. Something good must come out of all this chaos.

When I hear footsteps outside, and then the sound of the door being unlocked, I'm ready.

The person who walks inside never knew what hit them. I don't wait, just punch them straight in the face, and when they stumble backwards, I run.

Wow. Finally something that went better than I thought.

Now I only have to make it out of this building.

—ele—

I run, almost stumble in my slingback pumps that did a great job of completing my outfit. They do nothing for me now. I leave them behind with a pang of regret as I jog down the hallway, and down a flight of stairs. I must still be a little out of it, because I nearly take a header down the entire flight but catch myself at the last moment.

Part of me is a bit surprised that there's no one here, and Moretti's minion doesn't seem to try and follow me. What the hell is this? Were they trying to scare me? Alessandra?

Good luck with all of that. I have somewhere to be.

The building's exit isn't locked, and I find myself on a parking lot in an industrial area, close to the harbor. Three vehicles are sitting in the lot, one of them a white van. I still don't know how I got here, but the sight makes me shudder.

I continue, not sure where I'm going, the farther away from here, the better.

After what seems like an eternity, but probably wasn't more than twenty minutes, I find a gas station.

The moment I walk in, the eyes of the three customers are on me, and the teen behind the counter is gaping openly.

It's only then that I become aware of my hurting feet. I might be bleeding. I feel a little dizzy too.

Oh, and of course I'm wearing a wedding dress.

"Could I use somebody's phone?" I ask, and three people hold out theirs simultaneously. It's not that I've called Alessandra that often. For a heartbeat or so, I have no idea what to do, then I call headquarters and ask them to put me through to her. It's an emergency.

The person on the other side sounds surprised, but they seem to believe me, because a moment later, I hear her voice, unusually anxious.

"Mia? Where are you?"

"Long story, but I really want to come home. Could you please get me at..." I hold the phone away from me ear and ask the clerk for the address. He's still staring but shaking himself out of it.

"748 Riverside Drive," I say. "The gas station on the corner. Please hurry before they change their mind."

"We'll be right there," she promises, and I realize that my knuckles are bruised too. All that workout amounted to something after all. The relief is so overwhelming it makes my knees buckle. With surprising speed, someone produces a folding chair, and I sink into it.

This is not how I imagined my wedding day.

———ℓℓ———

When Alessandra finally arrives, Enzo in tow, she doesn't demand any answers, just holds me close. I still don't want to cry in front of all of these people, but those damn tears are dangerously close.

"It will be okay," she says. "Let's go home." She guides me to the backseat of the car. Once inside, I'm faced with an unfamiliar woman waiting, giving me a gentle smile.

"I brought Dr. Wilson," Alessandra explains. "She will check you out and decide if you have to go to the hospital."

She says that as if it's totally normal to have a doctor at your beck and call. I learn something new about the reach of the Falcones every day.

"I'm fine," I say. Earlier, all I wanted was to curl up under a blanket in my own home, but I'll be damned if I let petty people spoil this day for me, for us. "We haven't even cut the cake yet."

"And we will do it soon. Just let Dr. Wilson do her job, okay?" Her tone is still warm, but now in no-negotiation territory.

With a sigh, I lean back into the seat and tell them what little I know. I'm afraid once we get to the drugs, I won't be able to avoid that trip to the hospital. I was right.

At least, Alessandra stays with me through all of it, and when we are alone, waiting for the doctor on call to return, I cry a little.

"Don't worry," she says, rubbing my back gently. "Everyone is still there. If you're up to it, we can have dinner and cake as planned. I don't think they'll keep you here."

I used to get whiplash, seeing this softer side of her only for it to vanish the moment she went into boss mode. The missing links lie in her work, the atelier, and that incident she won't talk about. The puzzle is only starting to come together, but I vow to be patient.

Together we could rule this town.

I nearly laugh, thinking I might still be under the influence, but it doesn't matter as long as I'm here to cherish her touch.

Alessandra hasn't promised too much: No one has left. Oblivious guests have been provided with cocktails, and dinner will be served soon.

I can tell from Mom's tearful greeting and the firm hug I receive from both my parents, and Nonna, that they were in the know.

A lot of things about this abduction don't seem to add up, but Alessandra has assured me that we'll deal with it another day.

I have changed into different clothes too. If anyone has questions about that, or my bandaged knuckles, they don't come forward. I'm wearing flats with my dress now, eager to sit down and eat. I realize that most of the day, I ran on coffee and champagne.

But whatever Moretti's plan was, it didn't work. We are all still here, enjoying a celebratory feast with the people we love. That's all that matters, right?

Chapter Twenty-Six

Alessandra

No more patience. No more stalling. In the coming days, Enzo, Bella and I will discuss when and how to deal with Moretti's antics once and for all.

I'll make sure that Mia is at the table, too. She has proven over and over that she has a right to be there, and after how she handled herself today, I don't have a reason to keep her out of the loop any longer.

But first…The cake. Together, we hold the knife and cut the first slice.

"Some traditions can be fun, right?" she whispers to me. "I know we're not going on a honeymoon, but there's always the wedding night."

Yes, there is. I allow myself a smile at her words, eager to follow her line of thought though I've been watching her closely all evening. Physically, she seems okay. The circumstances of her abduction remain nebulous, though understanding who's responsible, is not.

"I look forward to having you all to myself," I admit. "And...You made a great choice."

"Regarding my wife?"

"Regarding the cake, but yes, that too."

The rest of the evening passes in a blur. Cheers, excellent food, not too much alcohol but enough to drown out the ever-present feeling of dread. We've met those challenges already. I've paid my dues. Seeing that Mia is fine, I can relax a little, an unfamiliar and somewhat unsettling feeling—at least when other people are around.

I seem to be relaxing fine when it's just the two of us.

Early on, I wondered if we had all made a huge mistake, but watching her interact with the guests, all possible doubts vanish into nothing.

She's at home here. Even if we had a situation just hours ago, Mia looks at ease, happy even. I tried my best to keep her at a distance. She overran all my boundaries, and I can't even be mad at her for it.

I got a wife. My favorite model and muse. A partner. Someone I might someday tell about Giorgia. I abandon that thought, not comfortable with it at the moment, and let my mind wander into more pleasant areas. Like the glorious sex. I got that out of the arrangement, too, even though I kept assuring her I would leave her alone. We were kidding ourselves.

I can admit a mistake when I make one.

Marrying Mia was one of the best things I've done with my life so far, and not just because as of today, I am one third of five hundred million dollars richer. Well, we are. That's another thing I'll have to break to her sometime soon.

Bella comes to stand next to me, glass in hand, wearing a happy smile.

"You are so smitten," she comments.

"Nothing has changed," I return, unwilling to share all the recent revelations. "I'm just glad she's okay. That was a close call. We'll have to react to that."

"And we will, but could you take five seconds to enjoy this?"

"Oh, I am enjoying this."

"Good. This is the only wedding I'll ever plan for you," she says, making me laugh.

"I'm with you on that. So, you're going to get your business off the ground?"

"As soon as we've dealt with the Morettis. That will give me extra credit, don't you think?"

"It will," I promise. Bella is the perfect wedding planner for people who also need security at their events. Silence falls as we are still pondering the mysterious incident.

"I'm so sorry," she says, her face falling. "I didn't mean...Raven and I coordinated everything, every single inch of this property was covered. I don't understand how this happened."

"They obviously didn't plan to hurt her. They wanted to mess with us."

"We don't know that," Bella says, and catches herself right away. "I'm sorry. Really. We'll go over every little detail again."

"I know you will, but she's fine. Mia handled herself perfectly, and she did all of it in her family's wedding dress. I know I don't say it often enough, but you and Enzo did a great job."

I didn't mean to make her eyes well up. "Don't be silly," I tell her. "Come here."

"Congratulations. You have it all."

Is that even possible? I wonder, as I hug her tightly. I guess we'll find out after we remove the last obstacle.

Since we were all exposed to a lot of unexpected stress today, I find it appropriate to take some of that cake, and a bottle of that obscenely expensive champagne up to our suite. I don't think Mia will ever return to that guest suite.

Mia. Mine.

"*Cara mia*," I whisper, putting a finger under her chin to make her look at me. She shivers, heat and anticipation in her gaze.

"I remember you promised me something..."

"Only if you're up to it. We could just..."

"Sleep?" She laughs and pulls at the bow of the blouse I changed into earlier, undoing it. "No. We haven't gone to all these lengths to just let the moment go by. Remember? Tradition? This is an important one."

Her fingers brush over the silky material, hands cupping my breasts as my breath catches in my throat. Who am I to argue?

Bella was right. I do have it all.

We pause for another sip, stalling, prolonging the excitement before we start undressing each other. No matter what issues we need to address soon, we'll have this moment to ourselves, this night, a sensual escape before reality catches up with us again.

I vow to make her forget all about the unpleasant interlude and judging from the soft sighs as I kiss my way down her body, caressing warm soft skin, I am succeeding.

Not that there were any doubts.

———

The knock at the door startles me out of a sleep so deep, I'm not sure I've ever experienced it. Regardless, I'm on my feet in a heartbeat, putting on a robe as I head to the door.

"Who is it?" I cast a fond look at Mia sprawled over the bed, fast asleep. The sheet covers very little of her delectable body.

"I'm sorry to wake you this early," Nonna says from the other side of the door. What now? I close the double doors to the bedroom and go to open the door of the suite.

"What's going on?"

Nonna looks as apologetic as she sounded a moment ago.

"We got a package this morning. Security already did their job, but you should take a look."

She hands me the non-descript box, and I open the lid, overcome with anger and nausea the next moment. In the box are Mia's shoes, the ones she left behind in that office building when she fled from her abductor.

"What do you want me to do with these?" Nonna asks calmly. "Is it time to call in our friends at the PD?"

I consider this for a moment, then shake my head. "No. We can handle it. And at the end of the day, it's better if our friends don't know about all the measures we'll have to take."

I don't have to go into any more details. She knows exactly what I'm talking about.

"Wait until you see the note."

"What's going on?"

Mia has come up behind me, her voice still sleepy. Her eyes widen when she sees the contents of the box.

"I'll leave you two to it," Nonna says. "We'll be downstairs at breakfast if you need us." She walks away, and I close the door behind her, turn to Mia and lean against it. I'm trying to gauge her state of mind. She held up amazingly well yesterday, but it's hard to deny that this could have gone wrong on so many levels. One way or another, we need to give a definitive response, and it can't wait.

I brush my fingers over her cheek, startled to see tears form in her eyes.

"He's such a child," she mumbles. "As long as they have some money and power left, this will never be over, will it?"

I put the box aside and draw her into my arms.

"It will be over very soon," I promise. "We'll see to it."

There wasn't a sliver of a doubt before, but when I finally read the note, it cements my determination. I have to go all the way, or no one I care about will ever be safe.

"What does it say?" Mia sounds a bit anxious, and I realize I pressed my fingers into my palm hard enough for my nails to draw blood.

She's no Giorgia, but I guess she will do?

I hold on to the note for a few heartbeats, my resistance wavering under her concerned look. I vowed to make her a partner, to let her in.

I didn't think the moment would come so soon.

I'm not ready.

Not yet.

I have to keep a clear head now. Him mentioning Giorgia, it means that I was right all along. Time to rally the troops for that final blow.

"Just his usual BS," I say, fold the paper and put it in the pocket of my robe. "I think we should get dressed and have breakfast."

If she's disappointed, she doesn't let it show.

"Then we'll get to work," I add.

Chapter Twenty-Seven

Mia

Hot and cold. Are we really back to that, only a day after our wedding? I refuse to believe it. Things have changed on a deeper level. First of all, they were pretty hot last night, but what happened yesterday, and how we dealt with it, means something.

I thought that day would be a lonely, sad occasion, but in fact, Alessandra's gaze on me filled me with pride. Like she understands now that I'm more than her convenient bride, that I can have a place next to her.

My mind is still in some disarray. I can't believe only yesterday, I got married, was drugged and kidnapped, punched someone in the face and escaped barefoot—only to resume the wedding celebration. Celebrate, we did.

I wish we had more time this morning, but I understand the urgency.

That, and she must be just as hungry as I am.

I talk myself into a state of less worry and more determination, and yet, she hasn't let me read the note yet.

All in good time.

I'm in it for the long haul now.

Some guests have stayed on the property, and so we don't raise the subject of yesterday's incident at the breakfast table. I'm fine with that, in need of sustenance after the non-stop excitement. I can't ignore the looks the siblings share though. The "getting back to work" is going to happen soon, I assume.

I wonder how Bella and Enzo will deal with me being involved more—not that the perimeter of my actual job will change that much, but I assume I'll know what they have planned as an answer to my abduction. Every once in a while, Alessandra sends me a pensive smile, but she doesn't give away much.

She remains an enigma, even after everything we've shared, and part of me loves it, loves the riddle, the chase.

Because it's beyond satisfying every time we come together.

My own thoughts and their implications make me blush, even more so when she says,

"You're far away. Care to share?" Her tone is low and amused, and I blush even more.

"Um...Not right now."

"Okay then. We'll meet in my office in twenty."

She kisses my cheek and gets up to leave the table. I see that Nonna has caught our exchange, and I don't know if her gaze is encouraging or sympathetic. Maybe a bit of both is appropriate here.

⁓ele⁓

For the first time, I sit in on an official meeting with my wife, and my brother- and sister-in-law. I've had the chance to study all of them in various contexts, and I well remember bubbly, excited Bella. Or taking-out-the-bad-guy Bella. Enzo can be patronizing or charming, but he's dead serious now. They all are, their demeanor sending a shiver down my spine.

I want the Morettis out of my life, and out of the lives of my family and friends, for sure, but I'm not sure what it all entails once we get there.

After all this time, could it be I'm still...naïve?

"First of all," Alessandra begins, "let there be no doubt. This was a ridiculous stunt by a petty man. We are all lucky, but I won't ignore that Mia got hurt. We won't let that slide."

Nods from her siblings.

"There's more. He sent this note together with Mia's shoes, where he basically admits to being involved in Giorgia's death."

I'm not sure how to interpret the glance that Enzo and Bella exchange. And why is this the first time I'm hearing about Giorgia?

Bella reads it first, then Enzo, her expression concerned, his impatient.

"Can I read it now?" I clear my throat, painfully aware that my voice has gone up a notch. Finding my place in this family is still a tricky task.

Enzo slides it over to me, and I notice Alessandra tense, though she doesn't try to take it back. Perhaps she knew she couldn't keep it from me any longer, hoping my reaction would be different if it wasn't just the two of us?

I read it, not sure what to make of it.

"Not that I want to make any excuses for Joey. I really don't care for him insulting me, but how is this a confession?"

"I'm with her," Enzo says to my surprise. "We do what we have to do. Let's leave Giorgia out of this. We have no proof."

"*He* could have left her out of it." Alessandra's tone is deadly quiet.

Who is Giorgia to her? And why does Joey know so much about all of this?

"We suspect, but the truth is, we might never know for sure," Isabella argues. "How about we come up with a plan first? I think Enzo's girlfriend can help us with that."

She smiles, and he rolls his eyes, another inside joke.

"No, stop." I nearly slap my hand against my mouth. Did I really say that? There's no going back now. "This concerns me too. In fact, since I was the one who was abducted, I'd say it concerns me a lot, so I want to know what's going on. Don't get me wrong, I'm glad you've been helping my parents, and Lucy. I want to be helpful too, but you can't keep me in the dark. And I'll continue to ask questions until you stop. Who is Giorgia and why does Joey mention her?"

Another exchange of glances. I shake my head.

With a shrug, Alessandra gets up to pour herself a whiskey, every one of her movements deliberate and graceful. I get distracted for a few seconds, until I remember it's only 10:15 in the morning. I think of the day I found her crying in the atelier.

Would I be better off not knowing?

What if she loved her?

"I think you can fill in some of the blanks," Bella says. "Giorgia was Alessandra's girlfriend. A few years ago, some family members weren't so open-minded. Some still aren't, but at least they know to sit down and shut up." She says that with grim satisfaction. "Anyway, you know how the Morettis operate. Giorgia's brother got involved with them. He owed them money. She died in a boating accident, that's the official version. The rest...We don't know."

"Like hell," Alessandra says bitterly before she downs the contents of her glass. "This is how they operate."

"They're not the only ones," Enzo reminds her. "Mia, you understand this is complicated. What they did to you...less so. We have to focus and come up with something to show them that we won't tolerate any of it."

"I don't want to send them a warning. I want them gone."
Alessandra's statement leaves nothing to interpretation.

Because of me? Because of her?

"So what do we do?"

"I thought you'd never ask." Bella is giving me a smile.
"Hit them where their business is most vulnerable, and in the
process, give a generous gift to the local PD. Now, for the boring
details."

I cast a look at Alessandra, taking in her stormy expression.
Somehow, I think she cares less about the boring details, and
more about a long-held vendetta.

How do I fit into this?

We spend the next couple of hours going over ways to hit
back at the Morettis, deliveries to take out, individuals in their
circle that might turn on them. I'm amazed at the wealth of
information they have amassed, and it's no longer a surprise that
they could act so quickly when Mom and Dad asked them for
help.

Come to think of it, it was probably the wiser choice
than asking Lucy, because it was never just about the money.
Alessandra finally returns to the table, and when she shares her
thoughts, they are calm, and calculated.

She doesn't mention Giorgia again, but her presence in the
room, a ghost, remains.

"In the coming weeks, it will be extremely important for you
to be visible in the company," she addresses me. "Don't hesitate
to ask us if you need anything, but do the job, interact with
colleagues and clients, make sure there is no doubt you belong
there."

"Will the guards stop following me to the break room?" I ask,
and for the first time since we left our suite, I get a genuine smile.

"You're not going to run away, are you?"

"Not if you continue to give me good reasons to stay," I return, and I swear Enzo and Bella nearly roll their eyes at our exchange.

"We're good, then," she says. "You all know what to do."

I represent, while the others take steps to dismantle Moretti's business in this town.

It's still a good day.

I remain cautious though as my gaze falls on the empty glass on the counter.

The riddle. The chase.

It's not over yet.

Chapter Twenty-Eight

Alessandra

The truth is that we had arguments all the time. About her brother and his dubious connections, about where to order dinner from, about what to do with a free weekend. There was a time when I didn't mind so much because we connected on different levels, but by the time Giorgia was pissed enough to go on that boat by herself, we were on the verge of breaking up.

In fact, I had contemplated going with her, not to save our relationship, but to get it over with.

I could have been on that boat.

I was going to break up with her.

Instead, she never came back, and that day, I missed an important meeting that almost changed the balance of power in this city. I missed a few after that, until I realized that Enzo and Bella would never be able to hold the business together if I wasn't there.

Sure, they have their respective skills and specialties, but someone needed to keep the bigger picture in mind.

So, I packed up my grief, shoved the canvasses into the small room adjacent to the atelier and carried on.

I rinse the glass in the sink, unable to push back the shame. I never let myself go like this, not even in front of family. I could tell Mia was concerned too. She'll do what I asked of her, but she'll continue to ask questions.

Some of which I owe her answers to.

I want another drink, but the first one is already not sitting well in my stomach. I can't afford this. There's too much on the line.

I didn't mean to stir up any doubts.

It's not that I'll go harder after him because I was in love with Giorgia. It's that Moretti making the connection means he would stop at nothing, and I can't go there again, not this time, not with Mia.

Perhaps I'll have to keep her at arm's length again until this is all over. Then we can have that conversation.

It will be hard, but I don't see an alternative.

Chapter Twenty-Nine

Mia

Alessandra keeps her promise. I am free to go wherever I want to at the company, without interference from well-meaning colleagues or security guards.

Today, I have Janet, one of my parents' project managers, over to discuss a new exhibition at the Museum of Fine Arts. We have contributions from artists all over the world, and Leonard Logistics will play a big part in getting the precious cargo to the desired location.

"Your parents are extremely proud of you," Janet tells me when we take the time for a coffee break. "They never fail to mention it, and I can see why."

"I'm lucky I have everyone's support, here and at our own business. It makes everything so much easier."

"Oh, I think Alessandra Falcone is the lucky one," she says with a wink.

I wish. I would like to make sure she gets *lucky* sometime soon. At the same time, I understand we are dealing with an urgency, and if we all play our cards right, we don't just keep the Morettis at bay. We'll drive them out of business for good.

"Either way, we should get back to it," I say, abandoning my train of thought for the moment. "We still have a lot to do." Making sure every painting and sculpture is in the right place when the exhibition opens, coordinating with the museum...It's strange, but I love it. A bit of everything, not so different from when I was still working for Lucy, except I don't get to be outdoors that much anymore.

That, I still miss.

Maybe, when operation Moretti is over, I could tempt Alessandra into a short getaway? It's not the same as a honeymoon, but I guess that would serve the tradition. I make a mental note to call Lucy soon and ask how far she is from reopening.

Before I get ready for another meeting, this time via screen, I call Alessandra.

"Hey, beautiful," she says in a tone of voice that goes straight to my core. I'm sure that she's alone at the moment.

"Wow. Don't do that to me when I can't touch you."

She gives a rueful laugh. "One could say I deserved that. What do you need?"

"I just wanted to hear your voice," I admit. "I miss you."

"Mia." Her tone is only slightly chiding. "I'm busy."

So am I, but I'm also worried. I'm afraid she could be slipping away.

"I understand. I won't bother you for long. Things are quiet here...I suppose, progressing on your end?"

It's not the kind of thing you read about in the news, until something big happens, like a bust, like business locations being closed down. We're not there yet.

"They are," she says, her tone a bit softer. And, so quietly I almost missed it, "I miss you too."

She ends the call before I can react in any way.

Back to work it is, then. But perhaps I can surprise her later tonight.

—ele—

On my way home, late in the afternoon, I drive by the museum. It's a courtesy visit, to assure myself the director and her staff have everything they need. She offers me a coffee and shows me around the premises, obviously thrilled about the upcoming exhibition. It's huge, a great opportunity for all artists involved with the Falcones, and the location is nothing short of gorgeous—high dome ceilings, lots of light streaming in, marble floors.

"We can't wait to see it all come together," she enthuses. "We appreciate everything your family is doing to support the arts, and the museum."

I smile, wondering if she has any idea what else is going on in our lives other than art. Probably not, and that's a good thing.

"We are glad to help," I assure her.

Art. Backdoor deals. Shady business. I'm lucky to have married into a family who won't sink to the same levels as the Morettis. Still, we have our secrets.

All of a sudden, the urge to head home and have a few quiet uninterrupted hours with Alessandra outweighs everything else.

I think I know what I need to do.

Chapter Thirty

Alessandra

"Look, you seem like a smart guy," I tell the man who's sitting in a sparsely furnished office in one of our properties. "There are various ways as to how this could end for you, but if you stick to the plan, it's not only the police that will protect you. We will."

Go for the weakest link. Our research has helped a great deal. The people close to Moretti are overworked and underappreciated, and after a few drinks, this one easily admitted to how he's looking for alternatives.

We've had one of our own following him for a while, and when she deemed him ready, she called Enzo to pick him up. Lilly confirmed the intel. And here we are, the gravity of his situation becoming clearer to Johnny Romano by the minute.

His eyes dart from me to Enzo.

"She's right, you know," Enzo says mildly. Romano doesn't like me, I can tell. He doesn't like where he is in life, but he dislikes a woman having power over his situation even more. I suppress a sigh. Sometimes I wonder how Kendall does it—but she enjoys being in people's faces, more of an extrovert than I am.

Until this is all over, I can't afford to let my guard down, be too close to Mia. At least I have a painting session booked for tonight. That should take the edge off.

Romano sighs.

"I appreciate the offer. I want to help you, okay? I didn't realize you wanted me to go to the cops."

"Not just any cops," I correct him. "Those who understand the special circumstances...Yours and ours."

I want to take a deep breath when he says, "I need some reassurances."

We knew the intel was solid, but people change their minds all the time. Out of loyalty, out of fear. Out of greed. But this man won't get any better offers.

"We'll take care of that, and then we'll accompany you to a safe place where you can tell your story."

"We appreciate it," Enzo adds. "You won't be sorry."

I want to roll my eyes, because he actually seems to believe it more if a man tells him. I don't. The sooner we can all go back to normal, the better.

<hr/>

I breathe a sigh of relief when I'm finally in my car, on my way home. This wasn't the first secret conversation we've had with one of Moretti's. Fingers crossed, it won't be the last.

The bust we provided for the local PD the other day was minor in comparison—once they have everything set up, this will be it.

There will be no vacuum once the Morettis are out, only Falcone territory, stretching as far as it possibly can without interfering with my distant cousin.

I'll have to send her flowers, because her tips were equally as good as Lilly's, Enzo's non-girlfriend.

I surprise myself by smiling. Is it becoming a thing for members of connected families to hook up with the FBI?

I like my version of the happy ending better, guarding tradition, determining the future.

Just a few more days.

———ele———

I have painted Sadie before, but it's not the same. She's fidgeting, and I'm starting to get bored.

"Why did you call me here?" she asks after almost thirty minutes of us pretending to play our respective roles. "You're looking for something other than inspiration?"

That couldn't be further from the truth. I wanted to paint, get a few more works ready for the museum, but with everything that's going on, it's not the welcome distraction it used to be.

Maybe I don't want to retreat anymore. There's a whole life outside this place waiting for me.

It's hard to pinpoint. I'm wound tight these days, and I can only hope it will abate once our police friends will come through.

I'm confident they will solve a murder along the way.

"I'm married, remember?"

"You're happy?" She's genuinely curious.

"None of your business. But yes, I am." The current situation notwithstanding. But if Joey Moretti wasn't such a pain, we wouldn't be here, would we? Mia and I, married. Falcone and Leonard, the pride of Cosa Nostra.

Kendall might have done something admirable, but that doesn't change the fact that she remained an outcast to some. I have different plans.

"Would you be happier if we were still sleeping together?"

She gets up from the chair, the short robe not covering much.

"Come on, stop it. We're almost done."

"What's going on?" a shocked voice asks behind us, and I freeze. I had forgotten that her fingerprint still gets her all the way here, and why would I change it? She's my wife.

"Sadie? Oh my God. I can't believe this."

Mia spins around and leaves the room before either of us can say anything.

"I guess the session is over?" Sadie assumes and picks up her clothes.

"I'll send you the check," I mutter. "Now, please, leave. You can let yourself out."

I've never done this before, but Sadie is friends with Camilla, and I think she has an idea of what would happen if she betrayed the NDA. I can't worry about that now.

When I make it downstairs, I hear the sound of a car, and I realize Mia is gone.

I text her right away. *Please, don't go. I know we need to talk.*

This might have been the first time I pleaded with her for something—outside the bedroom, that is. I press my hand again my forehead, wondering where she's going to go. Time to get familiar with that GPS app.

I'm stalling. I don't doubt that I can explain to her that I never meant to sleep with Sadie again, but I'm afraid this isn't the only revelation I will have to make.

—ele—

I see that she's on the way to the headquarters of Leonard Logistics. I pray that she'll give me a chance before she discusses her concerns with Flavia and Vincente.

There's nothing more urgent right now, and so I head to my car and get inside. I'm about to turn the key when something stops me. I get out and walk back to the house where I get my spare and start the car remotely.

The sound is deafening.

I allow the tears. They can't last long, anyway, but as I'm standing at the window watching my car burn, which might still be a metaphor for the rest of my life, who can blame me? With shaking hands, I pick up my phone and make the necessary calls. I can't have the house burn down too.

Chapter Thirty-One

Mia

It's a miracle I made it all the way to headquarters without causing an accident. I don't even know what I'm doing here. It's not like I can tell Mom and Dad about what I just saw. The pieces I put together.

To be honest, I'm not shocked about Sadie, but I've seen a picture of Alessandra I've been trying to ignore. How could I be so naïve to think I was the first "muse" she did more than paint?

Naïve being the word that sums all of it up. Alessandra never gives an inch, of power, of anything. The only reason she marginally involved me in her plans to get back at the Morettis was that they directly impacted me. She might care, but I was never in for a real marriage.

Her, painting a mostly naked Sadie, case in point. And I'm sure this is part of the reason why she's hardly been home. We haven't even shared a meal in days.

I don't know what conclusions I can draw from this, or if I have options other than feeling sorry for myself for a while, but I need a bit of time.

I head over to the office that's still mine, lower the blinds and lock myself in.

Alessandra sent a text message.

The unmistakable emotion behind the words breaks my heart, but I can't answer her right now. Everything is still raw, and I haven't even processed the abduction yet.

Sadie also texted, the utmost cliché *It's not what it looks like.* She's more Camilla's friend than mine. I don't feel like dealing with her now either.

I slump into my chair and wipe a hand over my face, frustrated with myself as I recall the past couple of weeks, wavering between hope and fear. Now, I'm not even sure what I expected to happen after all those secret plans had come to pass.

The truth is, as much I've been fooling myself, I still don't know her.

I know that I still want her.

That I love her.

That makes me the fool, doesn't it?

Mom knocks on my door a few minutes later, and I hastily wash my face with a tissue before I let her in.

"Mia! I didn't expect you to be here today. Have you seen the news?"

"What news?"

I'm stressed as it is, and I can't tell if she's excited or alarmed, or a bit of both.

"This has got to be the end of them," she says. "Come with me."

Is it happening as we speak? I hope she won't expect an explanation from me, because I don't know all that much. I did my job getting ready for the exhibition, as was asked of me.

I follow her to the office she and Dad share, a bigger space that also has a TV in it, showing breaking news on the screen. I'm not surprised by the reporting on major arrests in the Moretti family, but the somber tone of the reporter makes me flinch.

"It is yet unclear if the car bomb that exploded this morning in the parking lot of Ms. Falcone's home is related." She lists a number of incidents in recent weeks, including the arson at Lucy's resort.

I feel like I can't move or breathe.

"Mom."

How long have I been in the office?

What did I miss? And most importantly...Frantically, I pick up my phone and check again. There's no new message.

This is not possible. I think of all the occasions I simply went along with Alessandra's evasions and stalling. A car bomb. A fake boat accident.

Mom's hand goes to my shoulder, and she turns me to her.

"Sit, please. She's okay. Alessandra is okay. She's on her way here."

Her voice seems to come from far away, and I don't object, just sink into the chair she pulls for me. I'm afraid that otherwise, I might have embarrassed myself and fainted.

I still can't find the words.

"I'm sorry I scared you. They've been talking about the arrests for hours."

Hours?

"What's the time?" I finally ask, my voice still sounding faint.

"Almost ten, Mia. Like I said, Alessandra will be here in a few minutes. She was worried about you. What happened?"

There's no way I can tell her all of it, but at least I have more than enough reasons to be in shock.

"Where is she?"

"On the road, I assume. She called me when she couldn't reach you, and Tina told me you were in your office, so I came to check. Do you need anything? You're white as a sheet."

I'm fine. I think. As long as I remember to keep breathing.

"That was Joey?"

"We all assume." Dad has joined us, his expression grim. "It has him written all over it, but this time, he's not going to get away. The police have a ton of evidence against him and that whole rotten clan. We're so sorry, Mia."

"It's okay. I'll be okay," I finally string a couple of sentences together.

When Alessandra enters the room, not a wrinkle in her clothes, not a hair out of place in her neat bun, I feel like I can almost believe it.

"I'm sorry I couldn't be here earlier."

Mom and Dad leave the room discreetly when she kneels in front of me, taking my hands in hers. It is only then that I realize that mine are icy cold. So much for being okay.

"Mia. Love," she says softly. "I'm sorry."

I try a laugh that doesn't quite come out all right.

"Well, it's not your fault that someone tried to blow up...your car." Now, my eyes are welling up again. It's just been too much.

It occurs to me that Alessandra Falcone doesn't kneel in front of anyone—or apologize. Except she's done both of it in a matter of seconds.

"No, it's not, and we both know who was behind this. But that's over now. It's over. I swear. I know we need to talk, and we will."

"When?" I interrupt her.

Her fingers tighten around mine.

"Today. I promise you. But I'm afraid I need some food first. Flavia said we could eat with them. Do you mind?"

Before I can even contemplate the question, my stomach growls loudly, answering the question for me.

"I guess I don't. I'm just so tired. But I'm glad you're okay. On TV, when they mentioned the bomb..."

"Shh." She gets up and brushes a hand over my hair. "It will be okay. Are you ready?"

I nod, but when I get up, I realize that there's something utterly important I need to do first. I wrap my arms around her and hold on tightly.

"No more secrets," I say.

"Sadie and I dated for a short time, but that was over long before you moved in."

"That's only one part of it, but I'm relieved." Still shaky, but at least my knees don't give way under me. Moretti's nefarious plans didn't work. We're still here. And we'll have time to figure out the next steps.

A soft knock on the door precedes Mom into the room.

"We are going home. You'll meet us there?"

She smiles softly, making me wonder if she understood something long before I did.

Even if that's not the case, I'm glad the nightmare is out of all our lives.

～ele～

Mom and Dad don't have an entire kitchen filled with staff at their command, and still they somehow managed to produce an amazing spread. We have the choice between different kinds of pasta, pizza, chicken parm and veal, plus appetizers.

I can see Alessandra's eyes go wide.

"We were really hungry, but I can't promise we're that hungry."

"That's okay. It's a day to indulge. And you've helped us all a great deal," Dad says.

The air feels a lot clearer, even with all the arguments we've had to come to this point.

She hugs both my parents before we sit at the table, and Mom refills our wine glasses. It occurs to me that this is the first time since the wedding we're staying over for dinner. A late feast, at 10:45 p.m. And more than enough wine for four people celebrating the end of a terrible time.

I'm not drinking that much, aware of the conversation still in the near future, just enough to soften the edges of the constant stress and panic that we've all shared, one way or another.

Alessandra's gaze on me fills me with warmth and hope, even though I know she's not innocent in this. Her shutting me out made it easy to overreact.

I'll have to talk to Mom and Dad as well, but that can wait.

At least it's not awkward like those first interactions, and wine and delicacies aside, there are some subjects that are hard to evade.

"Speaking of indulging," Mom comments. "Are you sure you can't make time for a honeymoon? I think it would do you both some good, after everything."

I almost laugh, my mind still mostly in chaos. Joey. Sadie. The mysterious ex-girlfriend I might have never learned about if it wasn't for the note that came with the shoes. Everything. That kind of sums it up, and she doesn't even know all of it.

"I'll admit that after today, I'm considering taking some time off," Alessandra says, surprising me. She's always so polite, calm and deliberate. Calming me too. It's still unreal to me that our families decided we should be married.

And a miracle, that despite it all, we fell for each other.

"I can't wait," I return, and her smile is full of promise.

This time, I won't let go. At the same time, the need to feel close to her might override everything else tonight.

Chapter Thirty-Two

Alessandra

Since we've both had some wine, I call one of the drivers to bring us home. I was relieved Mia got over the shock, and so did I—I think—but she's growing quiet as we near the house. I can sympathize.

Where to even start?

It's a relief as well that she believed what I told her earlier, about Sadie. Despite her insinuations, I'm sure the latter doesn't have any problems walking away. I always paid her fairly for the hours of posing. The rest...It was casual in a way things with Mia never were.

I can't help smiling at the thought. Mia and her love of romance. I can't get away from it. I won't be trying so hard in the future because what matters is whatever keeps her by my side.

"Something funny?" she asks, intrigued. The divider is up in the vehicle, so the driver can't hear us.

"I'm not sure it's funny. I'm just grateful you're here. Still."

"Same," she mumbles. "We are really going to have that conversation, are we?"

"I think first I'll open another bottle of wine, but yes, then we'll have that conversation. I promised you."

"You did."

She holds my gaze for a long moment, sweetness and heat, and I'm hopeful that talking is not all that's on the agenda.

But she's right. It has to come first.

At home, we make a stop in the kitchen where I take a bottle and two glasses to bring upstairs.

So much for the first part. Now for the promise.

In my suite, I first start a fire in the fireplace, then close the curtains. When crackling flames provide a comforting background sound, I pour the wine. The events of the day are starting to catch up with me, I realize when my hand is trembling. Might as well get it all over with.

We are still here.

"Did you love her?" Mia asks softly.

No more stalling, then.

I sit next to her on the couch, reminding myself that this is the right thing to do, for us, so we can move to a place where we're both happy. Free.

"We were used to each other," I say. "Comfortable, at least for a while, until we weren't. I was going to break it off...during that boat ride."

She pales when all the implications sink in.

"I'm so sorry—I mean—You know what I mean. Sorry that you had to go through all of it. I'm happy you're here, that you weren't there when it happened."

"I felt guilty for a long time," I admit, drawing my cardigan closer around me. "I also didn't have much time to process any of it. We had lost both our parents a year before that. The Morettis were already smelling blood in the water, Enzo wanted to enjoy life, and Bella wanted to be a wedding planner." I can't help laughing at the irony. "Well, I can't deny she's very good at it, and now she'll have the chance."

"Everything fell to you," she concludes. "The business, the family...You had to keep it all together."

"Yes." I get up again, glass in hand. "I wasn't right about everything though. Come with me. Since we're doing this now..."

Mia doesn't ask. For sure, it was already clear to her we were going to the atelier.

I go to the door at the end of the room and open it, pull out the canvasses that have been hidden in there for so long. I was wrong about it. I was wrong to be ashamed.

And about how I dealt with it.

Behind me, Mia lets out a small gasp.

I take in the life-like image of the woman I spent more months with than I should have, reflecting a guilt I carried with me too long.

But the ones responsible for her death are finally being held accountable.

"I didn't love her," I finally give the answer. Not the way I love you. "After her death...In here was the only place I could leave all that pain aside for a few hours, and yes, I've made mistakes along the way. I broke up with Sadie rather abruptly once my siblings suggested I should get married."

Her gaze goes from the paintings to me.

"These are beautiful. I know you're exhibiting some pieces at the museum. Is Sela Andras too?"

I've been pondering this for a long time, and I haven't come to any conclusion yet.

"Maybe. I haven't made a decision yet," I admit.

"Why did you do it?" she asks the million-dollar-question. "It's all in your hands, and from what you're telling me, it has been for a long time. You could have said no."

Could I have? Possibly. Enzo and Bella are not the boss of me, on the contrary.

When I heard about the Leonards' predicament, I wanted to help. I did want the money. Those are the easy ones. But I was also intrigued and mistaken about what the deal would look like in real life. I thought that there would be someone equally as calculating, and maybe in need for evasion, on the other end.

Mia Leonard. Falcone.

I lean forward to kiss her lips softly.

"Yes, I could have. I'm glad I didn't."

"Why?" she asked, her tone a tad breathless on the single word.

"Because this marriage made both of us much richer. Safer, that too. I didn't expect to like my wife as much as I do."

"Like," she repeats, her lips curling into an amused smile. I almost get distracted, but I noticed that she missed part of my confession. I thought it had to be obvious to everyone. Apparently, I'll have to be less subtle.

I raise an eyebrow. "Adore? Love?"

"Is that a question?"

"No. It's the truth." I suppress a sigh. Much depends on the next few minutes, and me choosing the right words. "I didn't expect to love you, Mia, but I do. Regardless, I was always going to make sure you're safe. There's more."

Mia takes a sip of her wine, her gaze on me calm.

"We've survived quite a bit in the course of our engagement and marriage, and it only has been a little over a month. I think we'll be fine."

I'm glad. I can use the encouragement, because this, I can't control.

"Our grandfather wanted all of us to be married," I say. "He didn't live to see it happen, but that wasn't the point. Nonna thinks he was a romantic, I'm not sure. More likely he was a bit paranoid and didn't want us to bring just anyone into the family."

"Least of all, FBI, I assume. I guess you got lucky."

"So lucky," I agree, and then I blurt it out, "He left the three of us five hundred million dollars in his will, but the only way to access it was if we were all married."

I half expect her to jump up and run, but Mia barely blinks.

"Oh. Okay. That's a lot of money."

"You sound...surprisingly not shocked."

"I'm not sure anything can shock me anymore," she says with a laugh. "To be honest, I always suspected that it wasn't just about my parents' business. You could have just bought it."

"I guess you're right about that," I acknowledge.

"Did he know you were going to marry a woman?"

"I never actually came out to him, but that was never a problem with my family, my parents or my siblings. Is that—do you have any more questions? You know that we have a contract. You'll have a say..."

"Alessandra. I know. And there's something you need to know. I might have resisted the idea of this marriage before, but when I said I do, I meant it."

I stay silent, waiting.

"Alessandra. I love you too."

I sigh into her kiss, my doubts finally melting away in the warmth of her embrace, quickly turning to searing heat.

Enough with the confessions. I've cleared my mind and my conscience as much as I possibly could.

"Let me show you," she adds, and I have no objection.

Chapter Thirty-Three

Mia

I've explored different facets of Alessandra Falcone, some of them only making sense together to the mindful observer. I've let my own doubts and issues get in the way.

No more, and my gift, tonight, is to learn just another side of the complicated enigmatic woman that is my wife.

She has never opened up to me like this. I won't disappoint her. She will know that I can be safe for her, too.

Back in the bedroom, I'm undressing her slowly, kissing every inch of uncovered skin. I sense her impatience, last minute hesitation, but she doesn't have to worry. This will be just as good as the hurried encounters we've had, not quite sure where to go from there. Or even better.

I open the clasp of her bra and let it fall to the floor, brushing my hand over her shoulder as I step behind her to softly kiss her neck. She sighs with what feels like relief.

"I'll never run out on you again," I promise, my lips touching her warm skin again. I cup her breasts in my hands, thrilled when she leans back against me, melting into the touch. I let one of my hands skim over her ribs, her stomach and past the waistband of her skirt. That was just a tease though, and I can see the hint of impatience when I take it away and she turns to me.

Still waiting, though.

"Let's lie down," I suggest.

"Good idea."

The warm lustful tone of her voice goes straight to my core, but I won't be distracted. We remove the rest of our clothing, and once we're skin to skin on the bed, it's hard to slow down once more.

"I love you," she whispers, and there's magic in those words. Saying them out loud. Having gotten to know her in those turbulent past weeks, I'm aware that Alessandra knows the weight of those words, and she's not using them lightly. We've sailed past catastrophes so many times within a short period, we deserve to be here.

Every moment of it.

"I love you too," I confirm before I cover her body with mine, leaning in for a deep kiss.

More confessions might follow, but I think we've survived the most important ones, in every sense of the word.

—ele—

Despite the short night, we are up early for breakfast. With the Morettis out of business, there will be a lot more for Leonard Logistics, which means more busy times for the two of us. This time will be different.

We walk down to the dining room holding hands. It will be just the two of us—it's too early even for Nonna.

Which is good, because we have a couple more issues to cover.

"I need to be kept in the loop, especially if it's something I might have to react to, at work, or otherwise."

She nods. "Fair enough. I wanted to keep you safe."

"I understand that. And that will work better if you keep me close. I promise not to act like a brat anymore." I cringe a bit, remembering my first days in this house. "I did, didn't I?"

"You have always been extremely lovable," she says softly.

Diplomatic Alessandra makes me laugh.

"Right."

"I mean it. I understand those early days were...tricky. They were for both of us. So, you're okay with what I told you about the inheritance?"

I almost smile again, but suppress the impulse, because I know this is a concern to her. It's the sole reason Enzo and Bella came up with the idea, and now I think we should be grateful for it. If we were meant to be, it was this arrangement that pushed fate along.

But seriously? She showed me her stunning ex-girlfriend, I learned that she had a fling with my cousin's bestie, and both of us have faced life-or-death situations within days.

"I am so okay with it. Given what you did for Lucy, I'm curious to see where else you're planning to invest."

"Sure. I can give you an idea. An arts program for underprivileged children is one of those projects. I'll show you the plans if you like."

"I'd love that," I confirm.

Her face lights up, and I couldn't deny it if I tried. I'm hopelessly in love with her, the days of me being naïve long over. I understand it now, everything that comes with being connected, the parts that we might not like as much, what it enables us to do.

I won't shy away from money and power, as long as I share them with her.

Chapter Thirty-Four

Mia

At the opening of the museum's new wing, Alessandra has a space for her paintings, and there's one for Sela as well, a small selection of paintings with models mostly nude. I am bursting with pride at her talent being displayed for all the world to see.

Alessandra isn't one to engage with many people at a time, especially when it comes to small talk, so she says a few words to greet the guests and talk about her new arts program, and after that, we head home to get our luggage.

We could easily book a five-star hotel for a few nights, but there's a special surprise I have for her.

"Where are we going?"

"I told you, it's a surprise. I'm driving. And I'll give you credit for only wincing a tiny bit."

Alessandra chuckles as she gets into the passenger seat.

"You know me so well."

That might be an exaggeration, but the words still make me ridiculously proud.

"I'm trying."

She leans back into her seat with a smile.

About thirty minutes later, when I take the winding road leading up the hill to a more remote area, she sits up straighter.

"I thought they weren't open to the public yet."

"They aren't. We'll be the first to experience the new concept."

"Does that include goat yoga?" she asked, having me perplexed.

"What? No, I don't think so. I'll have to ask."

"No, that's fine."

"Do I want to know?"

She explains the joke Enzo made when he brought the idea of an arranged marriage to Alessandra.

"Okay, no. She's had horses before for excursions, but that's all I know."

When we arrive, Lucy is standing on the porch. She comes rushing down to hug first me, then Alessandra.

"I'm so happy you'll be the ones to test the new rooms. Mia, you'll see it's even more beautiful than before. I can't thank you enough for everything you've done."

I share a look with Alessandra. I have no doubt that Lucy is going to do a lot of good with this place. Not every action that brought us here, was by the book, but I have no regrets. Women a lot less privileged than the three of us will benefit from the stunning surroundings, the peace that has once again returned with the new and improved resort. I can't wait.

"You're welcome," Alessandra says. "You built something extraordinary."

"Thanks to you too," Lucy insisted as she shows us to our suite. "It's quite amazing how much good finally came out of this. We're so grateful no one got hurt, and that the threat is gone. In the end, we were able to rebuild bigger, with even more rooms."

We come into the spacious lobby area where I used to work sometimes. Being back here puts a smile on my face—being here with Alessandra by my side, my wife, means so much more.

I am better than I thought at what I do now, but the air around here is different, fresher. It will be good to come back every once in a while, and for the next few days, I want to introduce Alessandra to the beauty of these surroundings.

"This is so great," I say. "I'm so happy for you."

"Thank you." Lucy beams. "I'm happy for me too. A little sad that you won't come back to work with me anymore, but I understand." She winks, and for some reason, the gesture brings heat to my face. Alessandra tries to suppress a smile, failing.

"Anyway, let me show you your suite. Our kitchen isn't open 24/7 yet, but if you're hungry, your fridge is stocked, and there's a kitchenette in your room." To Alessandra, she explains, "Sometimes women come here with their children. While we want to give them a time-out, they might prefer to prepare something quick in their room. Everything is possible."

It truly is, I think. I saw a mysterious woman in a bar and fell for her.

A businesswoman.

An artist.

The woman I married to help my parents out of a predicament, to help her and her siblings access a multi-million-dollar inheritance.

We'll never know if Grandpa Falcone was romantic, paranoid or a prankster, but I'm grateful for him too.

"That will work perfectly. Thanks."

After she leaves, we start unpacking before I arrange some snacks on a plate, and Alessandra opens the complimentary bottle of champagne. It's too late for a walk, but I join her on the porch where we have an awe-inspiring view of the starry sky. I can see the wonder in her eyes, and I know I did the right thing by bringing her here.

"You like it?" I ask as I set down the tray. She brought the glasses with her.

"It's perfect," she whispers, and we kiss.

It is, perfect, all of it. Whatever challenge awaits us in the future, I know we can rise to it.

Chapter Thirty-Five

Alessandra

Mia's been joking about me not getting involved with an FBI agent, but the truth is Kendall is still important in our circles, hence our presence at the christening. I'm not sure how she managed to have it take place at the church, but she certainly still has all the right connections.

This event is filled with meaning, some of which we can address in words, some of which will remain unsaid.

For the moment, everyone is happy to admire baby Angela, named after her grandmother, who sleeps through most of it.

It's been an unusual number of big social events for me, all made better by the promises Mia whispers to me when no one can overhear.

I'm glad I made the decision to come out of my atelier, be with her in every sense of the word. I still don't enjoy these events much, but I do enjoy seeing her interact. She's a natural, and it helps to have someone in the family, besides Bella, who enjoys the representative part.

I saw Enzo moping at the bar earlier. Despite his denials, I think he had feelings for Lilly.

I sympathize, but again, this is a problem I could evade.

My gaze falls on Mia again who is engaged in a conversation with a woman I know mostly from hearsay, Sienna Caruso, and, as of recently, Joey's conspiracy theories regarding a kind of feminist Cosa Nostra. She's my age, and as far as I know, happily single, though there are rumors. There always are when it comes to women in positions of power.

"Congratulations," Kendall says behind me, making an all-encompassing gesture. "They said we couldn't have it all. We proved them all wrong, didn't we?"

I wonder what Mia and Sienna are talking about. Not that I'm jealous—just curious. She's a bit far from home, just like we are. Needing to be seen? To represent? Her family is in the hotel business, but what's on the surface doesn't always tell the whole story.

"We sure did," I agree. "Congratulations to you too. She's beautiful."

"Yes, she is." I ignore Kendall's knowing smile, unwilling to discuss something with her that I haven't even approached yet with Mia.

We clink our glasses together, and then I go to join my wife.

There are many ways to protect a legacy, but knowing who's by my side, I'm not worried about ours any longer.

Epilogue

Sienna

It's a good day. Joey Moretti and his father both received significant prison sentences, along with many of their associates. They're as good as done, and we barely had to lift a finger to do it.

I always knew that using Alessandra Falcone would be the best way to move the process along, as our families have never stopped talking behind closed doors about Giorgia's death.

I've felt for her. I have nothing but the utmost respect for her. But I must protect my own business, my own family. This is why I had to take specific measures to create an opportunity for her to act.

We are all better off if these men are out of the picture. I have some considerable challenges on the horizon. Friends can become enemies in a heartbeat, and eliminating the Moretti clan as a substantial player will level the playing field.

Behind me, Laura winces when she sees what's on my screen. I'm sympathetic. My staff doesn't get punched in the face on a regular basis. Usually, we go for more subtle methods.

This time, we couldn't afford to be subtle, though I'm genuinely sorry I almost had to ruin an ally's wedding day. Who would have known that young Mia has a mean right hook?

Water under the bridge, it is.

Laura was reimbursed generously, Alessandra did what was necessary, Mia stepped up and is creating her own destiny. We can all move on with our lives.

Back to business as usual. That's the plan...

About the Author

B arbara Winkes writes sapphic crime drama and Christmas romance. She loves writing characters who get the job done, whether it's stopping a predator or saving cherished traditions—while still making time for love. She lives with her wife in Quebec City.

barbarawinkes.com

Acknowlegdments

T hank you -

Dominique, for gorgeous cover art, brainstorming sessions, and sharing my life.

My readers, for following me from detectives to Mafia Queens, and back.

There's more to come!

Also by Barbara Winkes

The Crossing Lines Trilogy
(Sapphic Mafia romance)
Undercover
Redemption
Vengeance

Printed in Great Britain
by Amazon